G000116083

Sarah Clements

Rosie's Unicorn

Olympia Publishers
London

www.olympiapublishers.com
OLYMPIA PAPERBACK EDITION

A CIP catalogue record for this title is
available from the British Library.

ISBN: 978-1-84897-100-4

This is a work of fiction.
Names, characters, places and incidents originate from the writer's
imagination. Any resemblance to actual persons, living or dead, is
purely coincidental.

First Published in 2010

Olympia Publishers
60 Cannon Street
London
EC4N 6NP

Printed in Great Britain

Rosie's Unicorn

Sarah Clements is someone with two passions, ponies and writing. Her time is split between writing books and running a children's pony rescue centre. Her ambition is to one day set up a larger visitor centre and help people get closer to ponies, as she believes animals help us to create a better understanding of ourselves.

Rosie's Unicorn

Dedication

This book is dedicated to my beloved first pony Julian,
who taught me that four legs are always better than two...
especially if they are small.
R.I.P My big-hearted friend xxx

The Time of the Unicorn

A long, long time ago before the universe had come into being, a great god lived and ruled in the heavens, his name was Unus.

I don't want to be alone, thought Unus, and decided that he would create the universe; a universe filled with planets and beings which he could look upon and nurture. He decided to make one very special planet where happiness and beauty would thrive, filled with beautiful forests and cascading waterfalls, delicious fruit and creatures that would live in harmony. This place, he thought, I will call earth…

With this the great Unus brought about a gigantic explosion like a million flashing fireworks all going off at once which rocked the heavens. When it all started to settle you could see several new planets all floating around a giant glowing orb. The orb thought Unus can be called the Sun and this Sun will warm the heavens. Heat will be felt on earth and keep my beings warm and make food grow and flourish. But wait, thought Unus, we need water to let the beings drink and with that he leant over the little green planet and started to cry giant's tears. Whoosh they went into the bare valleys that he had created, making vast oceans and rivers and as he did this he said take my tears so that the earth knows no sadness and is nurtured by me forever. These tears I have shed will give life everlasting to your new earth my beings. He then went on to create the largest and most beautiful garden you could ever imagine with a simple wave of his hands… suddenly there were plants, lush grasslands as far as the eye could see, archways of sweet smelling roses in all the colours of the rainbow leading from one orchard to the next and every fruit and vegetable in all shapes and sizes with abundant waterfalls feeding every part of the garden. It was paradise from every view.

Unus reached into his deep left pocket and pulled out his hand to reveal one man and one woman. He gently lowered his little beings down into the garden. They smiled as they looked around at all the beauty and ran to feast on the lovely fruits and vegetables. From his other pocket he pulled out all of the creatures and lowered them carefully down onto the garden floor and opened his hand and smiled at them, "Go on my little ones, go forth and feast on the earth, be happy and good my creatures." And they all wandered off amazed at the beauty that surrounded them…

Unus then said, "Now, hear me all of you… this beautiful green earth is yours to inhabit forever, you must look after it and it will look after you, everything you will ever need is here right before you, all that you have to do is live in peace and love one another. I have made everything plentiful, all the water you can drink and the food you can eat, every creature and being to share love all around. But you MUST beware, avoid greed and selfishness or a peril will come and live amongst you all, instead of a warm, happy abundant earth you will have endless struggle and know sadness and fear. The way to everlasting happiness my friends is to be kind, giving and love each other, and to help you remember this I have a last gift to bestow upon you."

Unus then put his giant hand into his chest saying, "This is the beast of perfection, the essence of my soul, my endless love for you all. It is a free spirit and your friend, as am I. The beast will show you all the way when you are feeling lost..."

Unus then pulled from his chest, out of his beating heart a creature so perfect and so beautiful... "This is a unicorn my children, protect this beast and he will always be there. He will show you the right way and he will keep the earth safe night and day. He has the magic power of me within him and his horn will heal you if you are hurt. I give you this part of me to live amongst you."

But suddenly the fluffy white clouds grew black and Unus boomed, "Any one of you that harms the beast will send his magic back to the heavens to live with me once again, only once in a blue moon may he return to earth to seek out a being pure of heart with which to try and regain peace, goodness and balance on earth once again, only a child without greed and selfishness can bring this about."

The sky cleared once again, Unus thought, I do hope

my beings listened as life on earth could be heaven for them all and he continued to watch them all going about their business making little homes and eating the delicious fruits and vegetables and getting along happily loving each other.

This went on for a long time until one day the man being went for a walk. He walked and he walked until he grew tired and decided to stop at a waterfall for a drink. He knelt down at the foot of the waterfall and cupped his hands drinking up the refreshing clear water. As he splashed some on his face, a golden glisten in the rocks below caught his eye, and the man looked deeper into the water at the glittering rock. As it shone through the water, he suddenly felt the urge to possess the rock. He didn't know why but felt it could be very useful if he kept it for himself, the man had never seen this golden glow before. As he tried to pull the rock out from the pool he found it was stuck and it would need to be levered out. He tried sticks and then he thought, the unicorn can help me, he is here to help us so the man called for the unicorn and the unicorn came galloping to the man's calls.

"Yes friend, you called me, how can I help you?" said the unicorn.

"I want the golden rock that lies in the pool unicorn," said the man.

The unicorn looked down through his reflection at the golden rock and said, "But why do you want this? We do not need to possess anything here on earth as we already have everything we could possibly need."

The man said, "But see how it glows, if I take this home I can light up the garden when darkness comes so we can stay up later and eat more in the garden, why, surely unicorn, more of a good thing cannot be bad?"

The unicorn looked at the glistening rock once more and sadness entered his heart as he knew they already had a Sun and didn't need more light, nor did they need to eat at night as that was resting time.

"No, I cannot help you, you do not need the gold in the rock you simply want it and Unus warned us about greed, be happy with all that you have friend, and let's go back home," smiled the unicorn.

"No!" shouted the man impatiently, 'I want this gold and you have to help me, you are here to help us and help me you will beast..." the man then leapt forward and grabbed the shocked unicorn by his horn, but being a free spirit, the unicorn started to struggle and tried to get away from the angry man. "You will help me, your horn can dig the gold out of the rock and we will have light at night, you will do as I say, you disobedient beast."

The man pulled at the unicorn's magic horn so hard that it eventually broke off. The unicorn shuddered and fell to the ground and as if he had been held under a muddy rain shower the unicorn turned completely brown. His eyes went from glass blue to brown, his mane and tail turned black and his once pink skin turned to a dark colour and the unicorn just lay there drained. A darkness never before seen on the earth began to gather and in no time at all there was a cold nightfall. All the other creatures couldn't understand what was going on and they ran to their homes to shelter from this strange cold. Thunder and lightning came, heavy rain battered the gardens and muddied the once clear waterfall pools. What has happened thought all the creatures.

But the man was too afraid to go back to the garden as he knew he would have to explain to the others what he'd done. He had been greedy and selfish and ruined the paradise.

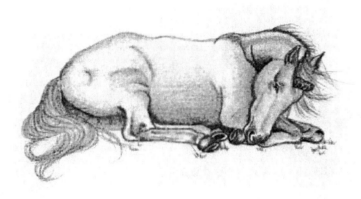

The man looked down upon the poor brown unicorn, his horn broken in two, and the creature just lay still in shock because of what had happened to him. The man nervously said with a shaking voice, "Oh Unicorn, what have I done?"

The unicorn lifted his head and went to speak, but all that came out of his mouth was a neigh. He could still understand the man, but now he felt fear and because he couldn't communicate any longer he simply got to his feet and fled now fearing the man.

Thousands of years have now passed, and horses and ponies are the descendants of this unicorn. They still neigh and they still fear man, but if you befriend a horse or pony and look into its eyes, it still possesses the spirit once bestowed upon it and if you are really lucky, they will be your friend as they were sent to earth to be, but wait the story isn't over yet…

When the next blue moon rises, a child with love and purity in their heart may just be the one to summon the next unicorn back to earth…

Chapter 1

In the heart of the south west there was a beautiful green valley, with old-fashioned villages dotted on the hillsides. The houses there had little thatched roofs and rose gardens with scent that filled the air as you enter their gardens and rickety farms where cows would cross the roads making you forever late for wherever you were going. This valley was called Homewood. Deep in the heart of the valley there was a dark, ancient wood and there in front of it lay a tiny hamlet called Edensbatch. In this hamlet there lived a little girl called Rosie-May Buckle. Rosie-May was like many little girls in that all she ever wanted was a pony of her own. Whenever she could, she would be looking at ponies, drawing ponies, playing with pony models, reading about ponies or watching pony films. If it had something to do with a pony, Rosie was interested. Every night she would make wishes to one day own a pony, every time her mum and dad would ask what she wanted for her birthday or Christmas, the answer would be the same... a pony please!

Our story starts just before Rosie's school summer holidays began. Rosie still had just over a week of school to go and it felt like forever, just waiting for the holidays so she could help farmer Trugg's wife with their horses, although, of course, Rosie wasn't allowed to ride them because they were enormous. They were all over 17.2hh and built like elephants, even though they towered over Rosie she couldn't wait to go and help mix the feeds and clean the tack with Mrs Trugg every weekend. They had four of these huge horses altogether, two large dark bays, a pretty dapple grey and an old strawberry roan mare, which farmer Trugg had owned since he was a boy. Rosie had asked how old the roan was but even farmer Trugg wasn't sure, probably over forty years old was always his answer. She had grey hairs on her face, long whiskers and not as much muscle as the others so you could tell she was an old horse.

In term time Rosie was only allowed to help at the Trugg's on the weekends so that she did her homework on time, but given the chance Rosie would have lived in the Trugg's stable yard.

Rosie loved the Truggs. They were kind country folk and they looked after the land and their animals well, Mr Trugg kept cows for milking and Mrs Trugg kept chickens and ducks which kept laying eggs which would turn into more baby chicks so she was always kept busy. They were always pecking at her feet or trying to follow her into the farmhouse, she was the type of person who would take in a sick animal and do her best to save it. Rosie really looked up to Mrs Trugg and Mrs Trugg was very fond of Rosie and treated her like a daughter. Rosie loved going over to help as the Trugg's children had all left home and gone to work in the city.

The Truggs owned nearly all the land surrounding the village and even the ancient woodland behind Rosie's house was theirs. Mrs Trugg always told Rosie never to enter the wood alone as it wasn't the place for children without an adult because when you go into the wood, it was very dark and you could easily get lost as many of the paths looked the same. Rosie had even heard tales at school that the pathways changed and the trees made noises!

This can't be true, thought Rosie, fairytales are just in books, they aren't really real.

It was a bright Friday morning and Rosie slowly sat up in bed and yawned as she heard her mother calling, "Time to get ready for school Rosie May, breakfast will be on the table in ten minutes."

Rosie pulled on her pink dressing gown and slid down the hallway to the bathroom. She washed her face and brushed her teeth and then looked in the mirror and said to herself, "This year something good has to happen... this year I must have a pony." The breakfast smell was starting to find its way around the house, so Rosie ran back to her room, got dressed quickly and grabbed her school bag. Downstairs, the breakfast was on the table. Scrambled eggs on toast with lashings of butter was Rosie's favorite breakfast treat, the eggs were from Mrs Trugg's chickens so they were always lovely and fresh. After breakfast, Rosie grabbed her packed lunch and her weekly allowance for a pony magazine and some sweets. She always got this on a Friday so she could eat the sweets at the weekend.

Rosie set off with all the other children from the hamlet. There were eleven altogether from her village, the school was in the next village only half a mile away, so they took the shortcut all together over Mr Trugg's field up the stony bridle path to get there quicker.

Rosie didn't mind school but she wasn't top of the class because she spent so much time thinking about ponies and not her schoolwork.

Rosie had a best friend at school called Millie. Mildred Critch was her real name, the other children would be really mean to her. Poor Millie wasn't very good at schoolwork, no matter how hard she tried. Making matters worse, Millie had turned up to school once with a large pimple on her nose that lasted for two whole weeks, ever since then the children would tell her she looked like a witch. The school children also saw her mother buying her a dragons and magic book as a birthday present from the local shop, that was it, they were convinced she was a witch! They would say, "We don't know why you bother with school books, you may as well get a spell book Mildred Critch, the pimple-nosed witch ha ha ha."

But Rosie didn't care how Millie looked, as Rosie thought as horses did, they don't care how you look, it just matters to them how kind you are and Millie was very kind, she wasn't a witch, although sometimes Millie and Rosie wished she was so she could cast a spell on the bullies at school. Far from being a witch or anything mean, she loved helping animals, just like Rosie, so the pair got on really well discussing animals whenever they could.

Pretty much every day at the school went the same. Some days the bullies wouldn't pick on Millie, but most days they would and each day they did, Rosie would help Millie stand up to them. "Bullies are just cowards, Millie, don't take any notice," Rosie would say to Millie.

The bell rang and school that Friday was over. Just another week to go thought Rosie. I can't wait for the holidays, in the meantime I can help Mrs Trugg with the horses. Life doesn't get much better than this. Rosie started walking for home, stopping at Mr Lovett's the village newsagent. She pushed open the big old shop door setting off the bell above, 'ring' went the bell and Mr Lovett came out from the rear of the shop to serve.

"Hello Rosie-May, what can I do for you today?" Mr Lovett loved saying this as the rhyme seemed to amuse him, but really he was a kind man, he just had a very funny sense of humour!

"I've come in for my pony magazine and my usual sweets please Mr Lovett," said Rosie.

"Oh yes of course, I'll just go and get your pony mag, you browse the sweets and choose my dear, here's a bag."

Mr Lovett passed Rosie a little paper bag with a pretty pattern on it, then went off through to the rear of the shop to retrieve the magazine.

"How was school this week, then dear? Are they still picking on your little friend Millie?" said Mr Lovett with genuine concern on his face.

"I'm afraid they are Mr Lovett, I don't know why they can't just leave her alone, they are still calling her a witch and she doesn't even have a pimple on her nose anymore!" said Rosie kindly, picking out the red jelly bears from a mixed jar.

"It's so unfair, but you know maybe there is something that can be done, I mean, what if it were possible to cast a little spell just to stop them being mean?" said Mr Lovett, raising one eyebrow.

"Oh come on, magic is just in fairytales Mr Lovett, surely you can't really mean it?" asked Rosie curiously.

With that, Mr Lovett walked across the shop, put the catch down on the shop door and pulled down the blind. "Don't worry dear, I have something you could only ever have dreamed could be true and I think you are now old enough to know my secret."

Unsure if Mr Lovett was joking around, Rosie sat on the little stair Mr Lovett used to reach things down from the higher shelves in the shop. He was wandering around the shop scratching his head and then said, "Ah ha, I remember where I hid it." He reached above the doorframe then showed Rosie a little key. "You must promise to never tell another soul about this unless they truly believe in magic!' said Mr Lovett, and by the serious look on his face Rosie agreed, fascinated by this point.

Mr Lovett then knelt down on the centre of the shop floor and pulled up one of the slabs on the floor, revealing a really old looking carved wooden box containing a little old book bound in leather. It was decorated with stars and animals, trees and a strange looking horse with a horn, and as he lifted out the book he said, "Now my dear, this is real magic." Then he lifted up the box and said, "I haven't shown anyone else this because to summon the magic the person holding this needs to be completely pure in heart, watching you grow up over the years my dear, I think... and I'm not usually wrong, but I do believe you might possess this gift."

Rosie looked at Mr Lovett almost waiting for him to crack another of his jokes, but he didn't he just held out the two objects and said. "Take them my dear. If you are the one, then when you open the box and hold what's inside you will know the magic is real, all of your dreams may just come true. The book will tell you all you need to know. I tried the magic myself, but I'm too old and I just knew it wasn't me as when I held what's inside the box, nothing happened."

Could this really be possible? thought Rosie. Real magic?

Rosie then asked, "But where did you find it, Mr Lovett?'

"I'll explain my dear. I was walking Dotty, my little dog through the woods to Pyrite Rocks, she started digging at the foot of the rocks and unearthed what's in the box," he said.

"What's Pyrite Rocks, Mr Lovett?" asked Rosie inquisitively.

"Fool's gold, my child. Pyrite is fool's gold. There's a

story in the book I've given you that says, once upon a time a long, long time ago, a god called Unus created a garden with animals, people and a magic unicorn to guard it all and one day, a man found the gold in the rocks and tried to force the unicorn to extract the gold for him, anyway, the god Unus took back the unicorn's powers to the heavens because of the man's greed and rendered the unicorn into a horse for man to keep on earth. The unicorn could speak to the people before the man accidentally took its powers away, afterwards all it could do was cry neigh as horses still do today," sighed Mr Lovett.

"If that's true, it's so sad," said Rosie.

Mr Lovett handed Rosie a tissue and said, "Don't be sad Rosie-May, the unicorn didn't die, he simply lost his power through greed. It's like life, when greed takes over the reason for doing things seems to fade, just like the unicorn's power, you see you may just be the one to unlock the power, if purity is in your heart, you can do a lot of good."

Rosie stood up and said to Mr Lovett, "I will hide this in the safest place, then when the school holidays begin I will open the box, it will give me enough time to study the book, Thank you so much Mr Lovett."

"I'll be here if you need me Remember," said Mr Lovett, seeing Rosie out of the shop. As she walked home so many things raced through Rosie's mind; helping Millie, saving animals and getting a pony of her very own... if Mr Lovett is right, maybe it'll even be a

Unicorn!

Time would tell, thought Rosie, time would tell…

Chapter 2

Saturday dawned after a rather unusual Friday for Rosie, in fact after the events the day before she barely slept with excitement, partly because it was Saturday and that meant spending the day with horses, but mostly because her head was spinning with excitement from the thought of what might become of her once she uncovered the truth behind what powers lay in the ancient box. How fantastic if it were true, thought Rosie, sitting up in bed daydreaming.

"Rosie, breakfast!" shouted her mother up the stairs.

"I'll be down in a minute, Mum," Rosie shouted back, suddenly the thought entered her head that she must hide the box so that no one would discover her and Mr Lovett's secret find.

Rosie slid out of bed and went to the corner of the room, she knelt down and squeezed her little fingers through a gap in the corner floorboard wiggling it loose.

The corner board had been loose for as long as she could remember, if you pulled it up there was a little secret hidden compartment. This is where I can hide the box, thought Rosie to herself, placing it carefully down and then lowering the plank back into place. It'll be safe there until the holiday starts, she thought. Then she carried on as usual going downstairs for breakfast with a glint in her eye and a knowing smile on her face.

After breakfast Rosie pulled on her Jodhpur boots, despite not being able to ride Mr and Mrs Trugg's hunters, yet she wanted to look ready just in case she ever got an opportunity to ride. She grabbed half of her weekend sweets allowance and stuffed them into her jacket pocket, nourishment for later thought Rosie, knowing Pip, farmer Trugg's old strawberry roan mare would eat most of the goodies.

Rosie loved old Pip, her real name was Strawberry Pip so they just shortened it to Pip.

Rosie dreamed that one day when she got a pony of her own it would be kind and loving like old Pip, Rosie skipped down the lane towards the farm smiling at all the neighbours doing their lawns and pruning their hedges which always seemed to be a Saturday job.

It was a good job she spent the weekends helping at the Trugg's. All that lawnmower din couldn't be good for anybody's eardrums, thought Rosie.

Rosie turned up at the Trugg's farm, hustling back the black and white border collie whose name was Nipper, as she pushed her way through the gate. Rosie had been told that Nipper got his name because one day councilor Digby Fox came to the farm to buy some farm land for the council. Nipper was a puppy then and Mr Trugg had started arguing with the man and as he turned to leave, farmer Trugg's dog jumped up and nipped him on the bottom! So from then on he was called Nipper.

"Rosie?" came a loud shout from the barn.

"Yes, it's me, Mrs Trugg, do you want me to turn the horses out for you and then we can make a start on the stables?" shouted back Rosie.

"Thank you dear, I'll be with you in a minute. I'm just collecting eggs, one of the chickens has decided to lay on one of those high beams, so everything's been delayed this morning," said Mrs Trugg with a giggle in her voice. How funny, thought Rosie, if you walked under the beam you might get an egg on the head, what a silly chicken.

As she turned the corner to the yard, the three younger horses were neighing and booting their stable doors with their hooves in protest that they hadn't been fed or let out, so Rosie grabbed the feeds and took them to the turnout paddock, placing each bucket in a rubber car tyre. She then ran back and grabbed the first head collar to let out Goliath, he was their biggest horse and was always lead horse at the hunt meetings. He was a huge Irish draught with a very dark brown coat and a slightly lighter muzzle, two white socks and a star. He was a gentle horse, but when he was hungry he could be very strong, however, he knew Rosie was small and was always careful around her, lowering his head to have the head collar put on.

Rosie patted his vast muscular neck and undid the bolt. His huge feet clopped on the cobbles in the yard as she led him to the turnout paddock. When they got into the paddock, Rosie slipped the head collar off and Goliath put his head down in the first bucket he could find.

Rosie went back and forth turning out the others, the dark bays were always first as if you turned them out last, they would be so raring for their food you'd be dragged on your heels all the way to the buckets.

After Goliath it was then Bruno, then the grey who was called Bluebell Woodland Surprise but called Bella for short. She was 15.2hh and had beautiful dapples, a long flowing mane and tail. She looked slightly thoroughbred with a hint of Arab, neat dark hooves and a pink snip on her nose. She was the type of horse everybody would turn to look at even if they didn't particularly like horses, she was quite young, farmer Trugg always told Rosie that it was best to buy young horses and bring them up yourself for the best results. He had bought her as an anniversary present for Mrs Trugg so that she could accompany him out hunting.

Last of all to be turned out was always Pip, she ate in her stable, being older she was a little slower and if she was turned out with the others they would finish their meals and shoo her away from her bucket and steal her food, but this is the way horses all behave, it's called the pecking order.

Rosie used to think this was unfair as it reminded her of the mean girls at school, it was what happened most days to Millie.

Mrs Trugg would always explain it so Rosie could understand. "You have to understand, Rosie, that in a wild herd there has to be a boss, a horse they can all look up to and be looked after by, with this privilege comes being bossy and taking food from the others sometimes, they do this to show they mean business, you may think it looks mean, but it actually makes the horses more secure as they know who to look up to," said Mrs Trugg.

Rosie understood once Mrs Trugg had explained, it still felt like being at school to Rosie sometimes but in a good way.

After the feeding and the turning out, they mucked out making all of the beds clean and neat ready for the next night, they scrubbed the water buckets and filled them with fresh water, then they did Rosie's least favourite job, the hay nets, Rosie always got in a tangle with the hay nets because the horses' nets were so big she could barely carry them once they had filled them up, but still, as she was trying to fill the nets she had time to daydream of the upcoming holidays and the magic that might happen... oh what if, Rosie thought as she pricked her finger on a thorn in the hay. "Ouch!" cried Rosie.

"You should be wearing gloves, poppet, come on, come in the house for hot milk and honey and I'll tweeze out the thorn and stick a plaster on it," said Mrs Trugg putting her arm around Rosie comfortingly.

Nothing like hot milk and honey at farmer Trugg's, thought Rosie knowing that there would be a bounty of cold carved meat under a fly net and fresh baked cookies on the table.

As they wandered into the house, farmer Trugg was on his way out with Nipper to move the cows to another field for fresh grazing. "Hello, Rosie, how are you keeping?" said farmer Trugg, grinning at Rosie with his fat pink cheeks while walking out of the front door, leaving Rosie poised to answer mouth agape. The funny thing about farmer Trugg was he didn't usually wait for an answer, he would just wander about talking and asking questions.

Mrs Trugg said it was because he was always on the go and he didn't have time to sit and talk. Oh well, thought Rosie and soon forgot as she sank her teeth into a fresh chocolate chip cookie that Mrs Trugg had baked earlier that morning.

Rosie always wondered if she baked them especially for her as they were always on the table on a Saturday without fail, Mrs Trugg poured out the tea and said to Rosie, "What I like about you Rosie, is that you are a child, but you are very grown up and I feel I can talk to you like an adult." This was another reason Rosie liked going to the Trugg's as she liked being treated like an adult.

"Rosie you know that councilor who Nipper bit before when he was a puppy?, Well the council has sent him back again to try and buy our land, they want to shut our farm and build houses so we may have to move. I don't want you to be upset but you may have to find other horses to spend time with," said Mrs Trugg, with a very sad look in her eyes.

"Oh no, where will you go? What about the horses? Oh Mrs Trugg, I'd miss you terribly," said Rosie, with tears in her eyes.

"Oh Rosie darling, don't cry sweetheart, sometimes things change and life isn't fair, don't let anybody tell you it is," she said, putting her arms round Rosie and giving her a big squeeze.

"Do you want to move, Mrs Trugg?" asked Rosie.

"Well, no dear we don't, but you see they want to build on the land and I suppose they have to build somewhere to house people and unless we can come up with a good enough reason they will force us to sell."

Rosie suddenly thought to herself, what if my newfound magic can help the Trugg's? If only it were true as there must be a way to stop this.

The day went slowly despite Rosie's mind racing from one thought to another trying to figure out a way to help the Truggs. It got late and Rosie set off up the lane to walk home, thoughts still racing through her mind. As she walked up to her house, she peered up the small side lane at the woods behind the houses. Oh woods, she thought, they can't dig you up surely, she took a big deep breath and said to herself, there must be a way to stop all this.

Chapter 3

This next week would be about the strangest but most exciting week of Rosie's life if only she did but know it.

Monday came, a whole week until school finishes for the summer holidays, thought Rosie packing the magic book into her school bag so she could study at break in the library. Oh, how will I get through the week without bursting with excitement? This thought was suddenly tainted as Millie walked over to Rosie crying.

"What's wrong Millie?" said Rosie, opening her arms to her friend.

"Oh Rosie, Emma Tong and Felicity Fox were really horrible to me on the way to school. They called me a witch and stuck chewing gum on my school bag, mum's going to kill me as it's a new bag," she carried on weeping hopelessly.

"Now, now, Mils, it's all going to be fine, you'll see, give it time, we'll find a way of getting them back for being so mean to you, believe me, Mils, what goes around comes around."

Rosie wiped Millie's tear-stained cheeks and, "Come on, let's get to lessons, we don't want to be late.

We've got to get through this week and then we have the summer holidays to look forward to, and I have a feeling this year they are going to be great."

"Why?" asked Millie.

"Just wait and see, Mils, wait and see, you'll know soon enough," said Rosie smiling. Suddenly it was like confidence had entered Rosie, she felt she had to try and help the Truggs save the farm and now the bullies were going out of control with Millie, why can't people just be nice like ponies are, thought Rosie.

All the children went into the school hall for morning mass. Rosie, who usually looked around the hall daydreaming instead of saying her prayers and singing the hymns, sat down next to Millie she wished and prayed harder than she had ever done in her whole life to let the secret magic in the box be true as she had a mission to put things right.

Lessons came and went, lunch break came around so Rosie and Millie headed for the library after lunch to read. They went into the library where the old library teacher Miss Sticks was asleep on the desk snoring with a spider sitting on her nose attempting to attach a web to her face and the desk to trap its supper.

She was at least 90 years old and had been at that school as a pupil and had never left! They crept past the old snoring teacher and found a quiet comer to sit in where the fantasy and fiction books were to be found. Millie picked up a book on fairy magic to try and find a spell to stop the bullies, Rosie pulled out her book from her bag.

It was so beautiful, made of chestnut leather with an embossed picture showing a man and a woman holding hands, lots of animals, plants and a unicorn, the title was written in old gold lettering with what looked like a vine entwined around where it was written, it was called 'The Time of the Unicorn'.

Rosie opened the big old leather cover to reveal an introduction which read...

For a unicorn to be real...

Before birth the mares' tummy has to be blessed with a horn from a real unicorn to cast magic upon the newborn foal before its rebirth into the world, each foal takes on the knowledge from the last unicorn to have owned the horn. It is blessed with it, giving it superior knowledge making it safe to return to earth, contrary to popular belief unicorns are never grey, they were extracted from the god Unus himself, he gave them pink skin all over like the colour of the palms of his hands.

As humans and unicorns were created to be Unus' representatives on earth they are alike in many ways, it is said their skin feels almost like a human's.

You can tell a true unicorn not just by their pink skin, but their eyes are glass blue like the clearest water to show the goodness in their hearts through their eyes which are the windows to their souls, their hooves are also always light in colour, white, pale cream or a yellowy colour, never dark.

Their fur must be pure like snow or soft butter cream, no dark markings or spot marks, unicorns stand out a mile from other horses and ponies and to the person that summons them they can actually communicate.

No other human has the privilege of hearing the unicorn's voice, after the fall of the original unicorn called Pius, which means 'friend' due to man's selfishness and greed it will be this way until humans truly amend their ways.

Since being struck down in the garden of paradise, occasionally a new unicorn is born back on earth, they have a weakness in sunlight which is why they prefer to live in dark places such as woodland, forests and caves as the sun's rays of light dazzle their eyes and burn their skin. If you have a unicorn you MUST, at all times, be wary of this as it will try and please you by following you out in bright sunlight.

You must never ever abuse your position as a summoning being, by treating the unicorn with less respect than humans as they are equal to humans, the unicorn's descendants, horses, became doomed by man's greed, they have to walk the earth without a speaking voice and to have fearful hearts. Unicorns aren't born fearful as they aren't scared of death, they know they will return again and again as it is their wish to keep returning to give the humans a chance to make up for dooming their horse cousins.

When humans do eventually make amends, all horses will be able to communicate with humans again and live in harmony as they were intended to as unicorns by Unus as it was in the beginning.

Unicorns' power includes a mind made in heaven, superior intelligence and the ability to understand all animal and human language whatever part of the world they come from, they gallop faster than any horse ever could. They can also heal and remove any type of poison with their horn just by pointing it and wishing.

Another of the unicorn's tricks is that they can change objects temporarily, but not themselves. They remain horse-like to look at, they are master magicians and can make a boil appear on the face of a person in the blink of an eye!

The only things they cannot do is be seen as unicorns by other humans, although horses can see them in their true form. To humans they simply look like horses or ponies and they cannot fly, even though many people think they can. It's because they have never really met a unicorn, so many books write the unicorn can fly but he cannot.

Pegasus, the winged horse, could fly and his descendants can also fly; Aqus Caballus, the horses of the sea, can breathe under water, another thing unicorns cannot do.

When the unicorn is created the chosen child with a pure heart must incant the spell over the foal holding the real unicorn horn over him or her and saying…

'Oh sacred horse, accept this horn…

and thou shalt be a unicorn.'

There will be a flash of light and as if by magic the foal will then grow immediately into a full sized unicorn.

Unicorns can be any size, they are usually around 13-14hh so that they can be ridden, but smaller unicorns have been seen in years past.

The summoning being should keep the secret of the unicorn to themselves simply telling their friends they have a special horse as the reason they spend so much time with the creature.

It is unwise to tell others about a unicorn as when people see something they cannot possess, past history has shown that they are jealous and try and possess what they cannot have.

If you are lucky enough to be a chosen one, treasure the creature as it will be your friend for life.

Unicorns only die naturally when their human companions own heart stops and then they themselves sadly die. This sends the unicorn's soul back to Unus to wait in heaven to be reborn again.

Lastly, remember your unicorn is not your servant as a horse would be, he is your friend, he chooses to come to earth to spend his whole life by your side, when the time is right he will show up in your life.

Suddenly, a loud ringing noise went in Rosie's ears.

"Come on Rosie, we have been reading all break and we need to get to the next lesson," said Millie, stuffing the fairy spell book into her bag. The girls looked at each other and smiled as in that break time they had both learnt that there may be more to fairytales and magic than just make believe. Miss Sticks was still snoring with her head on the desk, the spider sitting next to her admiring its handiwork!

The two girls giggled and ran past her to get to their next lesson. Rosie walked Millie home that day as she thought, until I find my unicorn I can't do a lot to change things, so to be on the safe side she walked Millie to the safety of her front door, then set off for home.

Rosie never got bullied as she had an older cousin at the school, this usually stops bullies as they are all cowards at heart. When she arrived home from school, she entered the house through the back door straight into the kitchen, grabbing an apple from the wooden bowl on the table and thinking to herself one day soon this will be for my pony… or maybe my unicorn...

Rosie smiled to herself biting into the crisp red apple, her mind racing once again…

Not long now, she thought.

Chapter 4

The week before the school holiday seemed to drag on forever. It was the usual end of term lessons and for Rosie's best friend Millie, it was a mixture of ups and downs as she had some lessons with Emma and Felicity. Rosie was sure they'd get their comeuppance during the school summer holiday break, but as yet that remained to be seen, you see, Rosie was not a vindictive girl she liked everybody and everybody liked her, she was so nice she would always stand up for Millie as she hated any sort of bullying.

It was the Friday when term broke up and all the children went to school in Mufti as the lessons were made up of fun and games and a huge end of term tea party in the afternoon. As usual Emma and Felicity waltzed over to Millie during the tea party, Emma said to Felicity,

"Oh, I don't think they are serving eye of newt and wing of bat do you Flick?" Emma laughed a cackle as if she could have been the witch.

Emma and Flick were quite sad in Rosie's eyes they wore the same sort of clothes as one another and they both slicked their hair back.

Emma had black hair and Felicity had blonde hair and was clearly not the leader, she just followed Emma everywhere and copied her.

Hence them looking the same everywhere they went, as the two mean girls sloped off to talk to the teachers with false smiles on their faces. Millie said to Rosie, "They really are like two greasy peas in a pod, I'm actually glad I'm not like that if that's what being perfect and beautiful is supposed to be like."

Rosie nodded in agreement watching the two girls suck up to the teachers, Emma giving evil glances back to Millie when she could catch her eye.

The afternoon wore on and school eventually broke up, the children flooded out of the gates, Flick and Emma caught up with Rosie and Millie.

"Oh no, what do they want?" said Millie under her breath.

"Don't worry, just stand next to me, Mils, it'll be ok," said Rosie.

Emma then stood in front of Millie and said, "Maybe I'll see you in the holidays, witch? Flick and I might see you dancing around a fire in the woods when you're doing your spells around your cauldron."

Rosie thought, yes and I wish you'd both go into the woods and get lost forever, that would solve one big problem for poor Millie anyway.

With that, an expensive looking four-wheel drive

vehicle pulled up and the girls were picked up by an equally horrible stick thin woman with a pointy nose who was presumably Emma's mother. She also had a voice that sounded like a frightened cat!

Millie and Rosie looked at one another and both said at the same time, "That figures!" bursting out laughing and running off together, the two girls got back to their village.

Millie lived at the far end in a little thatched terraced house and Rosie at the other end in front of the woods in one of a row of separate thatched cottages.

"Maybe I'll see you tomorrow then Mils, if you want to we could go to the Trugg's? If your mum will let you," said Rosie.

"That sounds like fun. I'll give you a call in the morning, see you later, Rosie," said Millie wandering off through the village picking at leaves and flowers from peoples' gardens as she walked into the distance.

Rosie decided to walk to Mr Lovett's to grab her pony magazine and sweets before going home, she also wanted to update Mr Lovett on everything she had read in the book during that week as by now she was becoming an expert on unicorns, all that was now left for her to do was find one!

Eventually Rosie arrived home in time for tea.

"How was your day sweetheart?" said Mrs Buckle lovingly.

"Oh, you know mum, the usual, it went ok but Flick

and Emma were mean to Mils as usual. I picked up my magazines and sweets for the weekend. Oh and is it ok if you ring Millie's mum and make it ok for her to come to farmer Trugg's tomorrow? Mrs Trugg is going to teach me how to plait manes and tails and Mils would love to help," asked Rosie.

"Ok Rosie, that doesn't sound like a problem, oh don't make any plans for Monday as I'll need your help all day, the gypsy fair is coming to the valley and I'm going to run a bread and cake stand to earn some money to help the vicar with his collection fund, so I'll need the kitchen clear on Sunday as I'm going to be baking all day.

"You and Millie are welcome to help, but you mustn't get under my feet as I have lots to get done," warned Mrs Buckle.

Rosie didn't really want to be in the house baking anyway, not when she could be at the Trugg's helping with the horses all day.

The rest of the evening Rosie spent in her room reading her unicorn book over and over, wondering if she could find the fortune teller amongst the gypsies who could tell her where to find her unicorn.

The next day came, Rosie and Millie met up and walked to the Trugg's farm. Nipper was at the gate wagging his tail pleased to see his young friends, they walked down to the stable yard to help out, even Nipper had a water brush in his mouth ready to try and help.

"Oh Nipper, what have you got there?" said Mrs Trugg smiling at the collie.

"I think he wants to help," said Millie.

"I don't know about that, young Millie, but we can let him hold it as he thinks he's being useful then," said Mrs Trugg smiling.

Everybody grabbed the feed buckets and placed them in the turnout paddock the same as usual. Then all of the horses were lead out in order.

Pip was fed in the yard and all the stables were cleaned beautifully, banking up the straw sides like puffed up pillows ready for the horses to get another good night's sleep.

When all the chores were done it was milk and biscuit

time like every other Saturday.

They all went into the farmhouse and Mrs Trugg pulled up a kitchen chair and said, "Right girls, this afternoon we are going to learn how to plait the horses as it's important if you are hunting or showing to present yourself well.

"We are going to use Goliath and Bruno as they will stand the quietest to show you, ok girls?"

"Yay," cheered the two girls excitedly.

Everyone drank up and ate the last of the biscuits on the plate then went to the boot room in baggy socks to slip on their boots. The girls ran on ahead and into the yard where they saw Mr Trugg talking to a council man who was just leaving. As he did, farmer Trugg shook his head and wandered into the cow barn looking quite sad. Mrs Trugg caught up, just catching the tail end of what was going on.

"He's a rotten man that Digby Fox, he's not nice at all."

Then Rosie thought to herself, Fox? Where have I heard that name before? Flick's surname is Fox he must be a relative, possibly even her father? How interesting, thought Rosie, meanness must run in the family.

It hadn't even dawned on Millie as she was too engrossed with untangling the mass of head collars in a pile on the yard floor.

The girls then brought in the two huge horses Goliath

and Bruno, they clopped across the yard with their enormous hooves, "Now girls, don't get trodden on as you'll get your toes broken," warned Mrs Trugg.

She knew that Rosie knew how to be around the horses safely, so the lesson in safety was for Millie's benefit really.

Rosie tied Goliath to twine on a wall ring in a quick release knot then moved over to show Millie how it was done.

Mrs Trugg then brought out two buckets for the girls to stand on so they could reach the horses' manes more easily. Each was given a mane comb, she then proceeded to give them both a lesson in plaiting for special occasions. The horses fell asleep whilst being beautified and awoke a couple of hours later thinking they were all set for a show! Once they realized they were just staying at home and had been willing subjects, they both snorted and huffed warm air in the little girls face's and relaxed once again.

One at a time they were un-plaited and lunged in the little sand school.

Mrs Trugg didn't ride out on weekends as she said the roads were too busy.

Rosie and Millie loved to watch the lunging as the horses would always give a little cheeky performance, usually a big buck or a rear in dispute of changing direction, the horses were very good really just a little spirited when the girls were around watching.

The day grew to a close, Rosie and Millie helped put all the horses to bed. The girls then gave all the horses a kiss on their velvety muzzles which smelt of oats and hay, then they thanked Mrs Trugg for having them. As they shut the gate they wished each other a goodnight and both set off in different directions for home, both girls going off thinking it was just the best most fun time and couldn't wait for the holiday to really begin.

Chapter 5

It was now the first Monday of the school holidays, by now Rosie had gained a lot of knowledge about unicorns and how to summon them properly if the opportunity arose.

Today the gypsy fair had arrived and was beginning at the other end of the village. Mr Buckle went off before Rosie woke up as usual as he was the village postman, Mrs Buckle had risen especially early because she was baking more cakes and biscuits for the cake stand at the fair.

Mrs Buckle was a very good cook, to earn money she would make cakes every week for the shop in the village, Rosie was proud to help her mum as her cakes were renowned throughout the Homewood valley for being scrumptious!

"Good morning Rosie, would you like some scrambled eggs on toast before we go off to the fair with all the cakes I've made? You know we are going to have to be there quite early to get a good position," said Mrs Buckle, handing Rosie a wooden spoon covered in cake mix.

"Yes, two eggs today please, Mum and this cake mix is

scrummy! Oooh can I have my fortune told if the old lady with the pied cob and carriage is there this year please?" begged Rosie.

"I would think that'd be alright, but remember, it's all a load of nonsense, so don't pay her too much money as you know she makes it all up," said Mrs Buckle, shaking her head.

Rosie liked the old fortune-teller lady as she had a lovely coloured cob mare who looked very healthy unlike some of the other gypsy horses at the fair, the gypsy lady had the most beautiful caravan of all the caravans at the fair, it was hand painted with scenes of places she had been to and animals she had met, it looked like a giant pretty horse-drawn bonnet!

Rosie loved to see it and to brush the cobby gypsy pony that was mostly white with a patch over her eye and a dark brown coloured bottom making her tail dark, her mane was white and very very long; the old lady would pick flowers and weave them into the horse's hair for luck.

Rosie bolted down her scrambled eggs on toast and went up to her room to dress.

She and her mother packed all the cakes carefully into a huge wicker laundry basket with handles on either side.

They grabbed a side each and carefully maneuvered themselves and it out of the front door.

Outside the garden gate was an old cargo trolley the vicar had left for Mrs Buckle to haul her heavy basket over to the other end of the village. They both plonked the large basket down and then Mrs Buckle said, "Quick Rosie, go and check that I've locked all the doors of the cottage then come and help me with this, I'll pull and you help me steer the thing."

"Yes Mum," said Rosie, running around the outside of the little cottage rattling the door handles to see if it was properly locked. She held her thumbs up and slammed the front gate as they both set off with their wobbly load.

After the tiring jaunt across the village, almost spilling the cakes, they reached the green. It was so exciting for Rosie to see all the gypsy horses and ponies.

Some had given birth to foals and were standing next to their mothers all fluffy and wide-eyed.

They set up their stand right next to the fortune-teller much to Rosie's excitement because then she knew she could spend most of the day in the company of the old woman's mare.

They laid out all the delicious treats, chocolate chip cookies, scones and cream with homemade strawberry jam, a huge iced sponge, lemon curd tarts, gingerbread men and the sickliest chocolatiest chocolate fudge cake you have ever seen in your life!

Yum, thought Rosie, let's hope I get a piece. Within moments of setting up the stand it was surrounded by hoards of hungry traveling gypsies and local people.

The crowd didn't seem to go for at least an hour

leaving the stand nearly empty.

"Oh Rosie, we should do quite well today, the vicar will be pleased. You go for a wander now, sweetheart, but be careful," said Rosie's mum.

"Yes, thank you, Mum. I'm going to go and speak to the old gypsy woman and try and have my fortune read then go and see the new foals, see you later and don't worry I won't talk to any strangers."

Rosie wandered across to the big old caravan with the old lady sitting on its steps. She was brewing her own hot tea on a fire on the ground, which Rosie thought smelt like old socks, but out of politeness thought better of mentioning it to the woman.

"Hello dear, can I tell your fortune today?" croaked the old gypsy woman.

"Yes please, I'd love you to," said Rosie, nervously as she thought to herself just maybe, if the old woman did have a real gift for telling fortunes, she might see if she was going to get a unicorn or at the very least a real pony.

They both clambered into the old van, which was actually quite big once they were inside. It had rows of old trinkets and what looked like dried flowers and horse hair tied with ribbon. There was a little table with two chairs where they came to sit. On the table was a velvety covering in a deep scarlet red colour, on top of which was a deck of cards with patterns on, to the right was a crystal ball on a stand with a thin veil over it.

Rosie could see it was her crystal ball through the material. How exciting, thought Rosie.

The old woman looked at Rosie and said, "My name is Mariella, please don't speak yet, my dear, I don't want any clues as to why you have come to see me, but I can tell there is a reason. I could see it in my tea-leaves you know... you have an unusual destiny, I can tell."

Rosie nervously played with her hair but kept quiet as Mariella had asked. The old woman then said, "I don't want to read your future in the tarot cards my dear, you are so young and your future is still being chosen with the choices you are making in your life right now. Yes, my dear, you can make your own future happen." The old woman then slowly pulled the veil from the crystal ball and began to chant and look into the ball as if she was trying to tune in an old television. She kept looking at the ball as if something kept appearing, then pulling back and disappearing. She looked at Rosie and said, "Its showing me a white pony, a baby white pony, a foal, not grey dear, this creature isn't grey," she kept mumbling. "No, don't be silly, that's not right... my old mare?" as if questioning herself, scratching at her head and looking up at Rosie smiling.

Rosie was leaning right over the table by now desperate to see what the gypsy woman could see. Then the old woman said, "My dear, I'm confused. I've never been wrong with my readings and I don't know why, but it's showing me things that cannot... well, do not exist.

I can see you looking a little older and riding a white…
a white…" Her eyebrows moving up and down as she
peered deep into the ball and then she went quiet.

Rosie said in a quiet shaking voice, "A uni…"

"Shhhhhhh!" blurted Mariella with a tear rolling down
her face. "You must never tell anyone if this is true, don't
speak out loud of this to anyone, it's real magic that I
never thought possible, you don't have to say it out loud I
can see the creature here in all its splendor, like the most
magical magnificent horse you could ever see. I've read of
this creature coming back to earth."

Mariella was shaking with excitement. "You have come to
me for a reason child, I'm going to help you. Take my
hand I have something very special to show you." She led
Rosie down the steps out of the caravan and around the
side to her old mare who looked very fat.

The old woman pulled Rosie's hand and placed it on the horse's belly and said, "Do you feel that?"

Rosie gasped with excitement, her eyes lighting up... then the old woman fell to her knees and said, "My horse, Freya, is heavily pregnant. Child this is fate." She then whispered quietly, "Do you have what we need?" pointing at her forehead, "You know?" she winked at Rosie.

"Yes, it's hidden where no one can find it," whispered Rosie.

"Good, good," whispered the old woman as she carried on, "we need to meet tonight. The moon is going to be full and blue just as it needs to be. Do you know of somewhere we can take Freya where no one will see?"

Rosie said quietly, "Yes, go to the opposite end of the village then turn up Woodland Lane, camp at the back of the end thatched cottage, it's where I live. I will come out when everyone goes to bed and we can take Freya into the glade through the woods."

The old woman then gave Rosie a hug and said, "Now remember, no one else must know of this for this to work."

Rosie then said, "What about you? What if you see, won't that stop the magic?"

"No," said Mariella. "It's ok for me to know about it, I won't be able to see it anyway because I'm not the chosen one, all I'll see is a pony, you'll be the only one to see it for what it really is."

"Thank goodness for that, well I'll see you later. I had better go and help mum pack up soon, I will see you later won't I?" smiled Rosie questioningly.

"I wouldn't miss this for the world," cried the old woman, happily stroking the pretty mare's forelock and kissing her cheek.

Rosie ran back across to her mum's stall. Her mum had started to pack up, as nearly all the cakes had gone.

Rosie noticed two pieces of chocolate fudge cake wrapped in tissue. Oh good, she thought, mum did save me some yummy yum. "Thanks for saving me some cake Mum. I had my fortune told but there was nothing much I didn't already know. Oh, Mariella is going to park her horse-drawn van in Woodland Lane as her mare is heavily pregnant and needs peace and quiet, that is ok isn't it?" asked Rosie.

"Of course, Rosie, but only Mariella as we have known she has been with the traveling fair for years. It's important never to invite people you don't know near to the house, but you're a sensible girl," said Mrs Buckle, stroking Rosie's cheek.

They continued to pack up and loaded the basket back onto the trolley which was now considerably lighter than when they set out. As Rosie wandered back though the village helping her mum steer the trolley, she remembered she hadn't seen any of the other gypsy foals. This time it didn't matter to Rosie, as she was too busy dreaming of what might happen later on that night.

All she needed now was to wait for everyone to go to bed and for a blue moon to rise. She didn't know how she would ever cope with having to wait, as she was filled with excitement at the thought of seeing the birth of her future, her very own unicorn friend.

Chapter 6

It was still the day of the fair and it had been a long day already for little Rosie-May, but she was still full of energy driven by the excitement of the thought of what might still happen that night.

It was getting dark and nearly time for bed. Rosie turned to her mother and father and told them she was getting an early night, she then headed for her bedroom, closing the door tightly behind her.

She removed her shoes, took out her pyjamas from under her pillow and put them on over her clothes. She climbed into bed and put her bedside table lamp on then switched the main bedroom light off, just leaving her enough light so she could have another read through of her unicorn summoning book to make sure she knew it all off by heart.

When she finally heard her parents coming up the stairs, she turned off her bedside lamp and pretended to be asleep. From squinting eyes she saw her mother open the door and look in to check on her.

Then Rosie just lay in wait. It came to past midnight and she could hear her father snoring loudly. They were asleep at last, she thought.

Very quietly pulling back the covers, she stood up and removed her pyjamas then crept to the corner of the room trying not to make a sound.

She poked her small fingers through the little gap and wiggled the board up to reveal the little box. She lifted it out carefully and replaced the board. Very quietly she turned her bedroom door handle and opened it slowly so that it wouldn't creak.

She picked up her shoes in the other hand and then scurried quietly down the hall and tiptoed down the old staircase. Rosie had never done anything naughty like this before and was a little bit scared, she decided to leave a note just in case her parents found her not there and panicked.

She left the note in the bread-bin, it was the first thing they touched in the morning and she knew she would be back before then, so she could remove the note on her return.

Rosie then grabbed some biscuits and crept out of the house with the box clasped tightly to her chest under her jacket.

Rosie crept to the back of the garden and climbed over the wall as she knew the front gate hinge would squeak loudly and her parents might wake up.

Rosie tapped on the side of the caravan and out came the old woman with a beaming smile. "Right, my child, are you ready for this? We need to lead Freya into the woods where she can't be seen."

Rosie nodded her head, the old woman climbed down the little steps. They both went to the rear of the van where Freya was quietly eating some grass in the lane.

The old woman grabbed her head collar and attached a shorter rope then they all headed off into the woods.

It was so bright, the moon was starting to shine through the clouds and light up the way. Not far into the wood was a glade, a clearing where light shone through and when you looked up you could clearly see the moon and the stars.

They got to the clearing and stopped. "Right, child, you know what to do, don't be scared I'm here with you," said Mariella.

Rosie then nervously opened her coat and pulled out the leather covered box. She opened it carefully and pulled out a small object wrapped in old parchment cloth, the object started to shake, but Rosie carried on opening the layers of parchment until she uncovered what looked like an ancient horn.

"It's the last living unicorn's horn, child," said Mariella excitedly. Rosie then placed the horn onto her palm and looked at it. With that, a sudden blinding light came out of the horn, it shone all around as if she were holding a star that had fallen from the night sky lighting up the whole glade. "Don't let go, child, this means you are the true chosen one."

Rosie then stroked the horn across Freya's tummy and then the horse quietly lay down. She started to make noises as if she were trying to push. The old woman and Rosie then watched the mare give birth. Out came the little foal, the mare cleaned him up like all good mother horses do and helped him get to his feet. Rosie and Mariella stood aside as the mother and baby spent their first moments together. The foal was pure white, with little white hooves and big blue eyes.

Rosie whispered to the old woman, "Do you really think this is going to work?"

"We'll see, won't we? Let him drink his fill from his mummy. The first drink will help him stay protected, then you can try the spell." They sat and watched the little colt jump around and learn to stand on his legs then he drank and he drank and he drank.

Feeling full, the little white colt lay down near his mother. Rosie timidly went over to the colt and sat by his side. She held out her hand and stroked his tiny pink nose.

It was like velvet and she could see as the moon shone upon him his clear blue eyes almost like shimmering glass pools.

Rosie had never seen such a beautiful little thing. It was then that she quietly pulled out the unicorn horn once again and wished with all her might that real magic would really happen here and now. She held the horn over the little colt's head and said the turning spell...

"Oh sacred horse, accept this horn and thou shalt be a unicorn..."

Suddenly the horn attached itself to the foal's forehead and a swirling mist covered the foal. Rosie moved back, a little afraid but very excited. Before her eyes she then witnessed the most miraculous thing she ever thought possible, the foal started to grow at a rapid pace, he filled out and his mane and tail grew long and beautiful. He grew and grew until he was almost the same size as full sized little horse.

He then struggled to his feet and looked at his mother,

who was resting on the ground with Mariella asleep next to her.

Then Rosie heard a voice. "They weren't allowed to see me change Rosie, that's why they are asleep and when they wake up, Mariella the old woman won't see me as you do, she won't hear me either. You know I cannot live in sunlight, don't you, Rosie?" said the unicorn.

Rosie stood there in shock, but then realised this was real and spoke to her new friend nervously, "Y-y-y-yes I know that. If you spend time in the sun you will burn and that you cannot see well in daylight, so we need to find you a place to live, somewhere in these woods," said Rosie.

"I know a place here in the woods," said the unicorn.

"How do you know? You have just been born? And what is your name?" Rosie fired the questions at the unicorn.

"Well, I know a place I can hide for now, because I have lived here before, many lives and moons ago. You are forgetting that every horse that has become a unicorn has lived a life and imprinted their life time's memory into the horn, I now possess these memories so I can find the place, I have been there many times before except as another unicorn, Unus said my name in this life is to be Image. He names every one of us before we are conceived," smiled the unicorn at Rosie.

"That's a lovely name," smiled Rosie at her new

friend.

"I had better go and find my old home and make sure it's safe. You and Mariella ought to go and have a cup of tea and those biscuits you brought out," said the unicorn.

"How did you know about the biscuits?" asked Rosie.

"I was inside my mum's tummy but I could hear you!" said the unicorn giggling.

Rosie then turned to the unicorn, "How will I find you again Image?"

The unicorn turned to her and said, "You just shut your eyes and say my name inside your head three times and I will find you. You will need to find me a bit-less bridle so people don't think it's odd you having a loose horse following you around, so Rosie that's your little project until next time I see you.

Give me a day to rest and then call for me, oh and could you bring something nice to eat? I'm unsure what they are, but my mind is telling me I like carrots and apples, whatever they might be," said the unicorn looking a little confused.

"How about sugar lumps?" asked Rosie.

"I don't even know what carrots and apples are, but bring the lumps as well and I'll try them. I've only just got used to milk!" laughed the unicorn.

He then went over to his mother and kissed her cheek and said, "Wake up now, Mother." And the mare lifted her head and looked at her somewhat larger baby. You could tell she knew it was her baby as she nuzzled into him.

"Mother, I have to leave you as I am now a unicorn, thank you for bringing me to earth, go with Mariella and don't be sad to lose me, I will see you again I'm sure."

With that the old mare stood up and started licking the old woman's face. Rosie knelt down and gently shook the old woman until her eyes opened. "Wake up, you missed it all, but it worked."

The old woman looked at the big white pony standing next to her mare. "Oh my goodness, it's really true! Well he's a free spirit now and you, my child have a friend for life and a destiny to follow. I'm sorry I went to sleep I don't quite know what happened there. I must have nodded off." Mariella scratched her head, still wondering what had happened.

"It's alright, you just weren't allowed to see him change," said Rosie, holding out her hand to help the old woman to her feet.

She stood up and wiped the grass from her skirt. She cupped the little white pony's face and said, "Look after this little girl, she's a sweet child and I will see you again, I hope." She kissed the unicorn on the nose and stroked his cheek.

The unicorn then turned to Rosie and said, "She can't hear me, but thank her and tell her I hope we meet again in this life or the next. Tell her to look after my mother for me and yes, I will look after you, Rosie." And with that, the unicorn gave Rosie a big wet horsey kiss on the cheek and galloped off into the dark woods, slowly vanishing into the darkness.

"Right then madam, we had better get you home before someone realises you're gone, but what a night, I still can't believe I fell asleep," said Mariella to Rosie.

They got back to the cottage and Rosie jumped over the wall. "See you again Rosie, bye bye." Mariella waved as she left.

Rosie then crept into the house and removed the note, and sneaked up to her bedroom. No sooner had she undressed and got into bed, she could then hear her father get up for his postal round. Phew! That was close, thought Rosie, but so worth it.

Life is going to be magic from now on, I just know it.

Chapter 7

It was the morning after the night before and Rosie had only had a couple of hours sleep. Usually in the holidays, she would be up early and either running around to Millie's or going to the Trugg's to help with the horses, but she had been up all night and was very tired.

Her mum came up the stairs with a warm cocoa and tapped on the door. "Good morning, sleepyhead, it's not like you to sleep in during the holidays. Are you feeling alright?" said her mother, leaning over Rosie and feeling her forehead.

Rosie hated lying and said, "Yesterday's events must have worn me out, Mum." So technically she wasn't lying, but she knew she had to conceal the truth for if she had said she was out all night with a gypsy woman creating a unicorn, she would surely be grounded for lying and that was a fact!

Exceptional circumstances call for exceptional measures, thought Rosie, as no one must find out about Image under any circumstance.

"Alright, well, you have a lie-in and then I'll make you a late breakfast. I believe the Truggs are expecting you, I had better pop down and tell them you won't be down until this afternoon, alright?" asked Rosie's mum.

Rosie nodded at her mother and snuggled back under her warm duvet. Thank goodness for that, thought Rosie, I am so tired. She nodded back off to sleep, her cocoa going cold on the bedside cabinet next to her.

Rosie awoke at lunchtime to the smell of cooking. She turned to her cup of now cold cocoa and took a sip, it was still nice as it had gone cold and had turned into chocolate milkshake so she finished it off and sat up yawning.

I wonder what's going to happen today thought Rosie, wondering if the night before had been real. She climbed out of bed slowly, washed and dressed then trundled down the stairs to the now delicious smelling kitchen.

"You were too late for breakfast, so I started making a roast lunch, so come along, sit up and tuck in," said Rosie's mum.

Yum, thought Rosie, just what I need, a good meal before today's adventures. There was a tap at the door and Millie popped her head around the half open front door.

"Hi Millie, come on in, would you like some lunch as I'm just serving up a roast," asked Rosie's mum.

"Oh, yes please, I am rather hungry. Mum went to work and I was left with the ingredients for cheese sandwiches, so that'll be really nice, thank you very much, Mrs Buckle," said Millie pulling up a creaky chair opposite Rosie.

The girls tucked into their roasts with hungry haste then got slower and slower as they filled up their little tummies. Mrs Buckle always overloaded plates as she liked to see people eat well.

Rosie and Millie looked at each other over the plates still with some food on them, their tummies feeling as if they would burst. "Mum, I can't eat anymore and I think Millie's had enough, may we finish please?'

Mrs Buckle looked at the two little girls holding their tummies. Millie undoing the top button of her jeans so she could breath. "Ok girls, I suppose I did give you man sized portions, you go and relax in your bedroom for a while then set off for farmer Trugg's," she laughed.

The girls then left the table and went up to Rosie's bedroom. Rosie shut the door and both the girls sat on the bed. "I have a secret to tell you Millie, but you must promise not to tell anyone ever."

Millie sat up interestedly. "Oh tell me, I promise, I promise."

Rosie thought I'll have to tell Millie I have a pony, otherwise she'll suspect something. Oh I hate to lie, but I must conceal the truth as it says in the book.

She then turned to Millie and said, "Yesterday I helped mum at the gypsy fair and the fortune-teller lady gave me a pony. Mum doesn't know, so I'm keeping him in the woods, he has no skin pigment you see and needs to be in the dark and that's why the gypsy gave him to me, she just couldn't travel with him in the daytime."

Millie gasped. "Wow, really? Your own pony, but if you leave him in the woods won't he run away?" asked a rather confused Millie.

"No, he's a gypsy pony and is used to being left in strange places, but we need to go and feed him later," said Rosie.

"But Rosie, we aren't supposed to go into the woods alone, it might be dangerous and we might get lost," said Millie, chewing on her bottom lip.

"Well, we'll be together. Come on, this is my only chance ever to have a pony of my own, please come with me, we can gather him some food after we have mucked out at the Trugg's," said Rosie.

"Alright but don't leave me on my own, Rosie, I'm scared of being left in the woods. I've heard stories at school about the pathway disappearing and strange things happening in those woods," shook Millie.

"They're just stories, Millie, probably started by Emma or Flick just to scare you. We'll be fine, I just know it," said Rosie, trying to sound convincing.

The two girls then headed back down to the kitchen where Mrs Buckle was just finishing the washing up. "I'll see you later Rosie. You both be careful, here's some apple and carrots cuttings for Mrs Trugg's horses in this bag. Oh, and you have an envelope here addressed to you, Rosie," said her mother, passing her the bag and the envelope.

"Thanks, Mum." Rosie took the envelope and wandered into the hall to pull on her boots.

"What do you think that is?" asked Millie.

"I don't know, we'll read it outside, come on," said Rosie, leading Millie into the garden.

She tore open the envelope and a bracelet slipped out onto her hand. It looked like a charm bracelet. Rosie pulled out the letter and it read...

Dearest Rosie,

Keep this letter safe, it is to say that I gave you 'Image' the pony so you own him. This will stop anyone that tries to take him away from you, he is totally yours and no one else has any right over him except you.

I'm afraid I have sad news. I didn't tell you yesterday because I didn't want to ruin your special moment. I am afraid I am very ill, when the time comes I want to leave you my horse and carriage. It may be soon or it may be a number of years, but I am going to stay on the road for as long as I can, as it's my wish to do so.

I never had any children so I want to hand my worldly goods to you, my child. Don't be sad, don't even cry as we all come back again to this world after we die, so even if I leave soon I know I will be safe.

In life things aren't always fair Rosie, but you need to think positively whatever happens, as what you think will be drawn to you, the good and the bad. Look after Image as I know he will look after you, use him wisely and listen to his wisdom, it will help you through difficult times in life. I now bid you farewell, enjoy my carriage when it comes to you, look after Freya, she has a good many years also left in her, many magical secrets are stored within the old carriage itself, discover them and take care.

Signed Mariella Maria Romaneska

PS. keep this horsehair charm bracelet. It will bring you luck and is made from Images' mother's hair so you

also have something of hers until the day she and my
carriage turn up at your door for you to keep.

Rosie felt upset as it was a bittersweet letter. She didn't want Mariella to die as she was so kind and friendly, but it helped that she had explained to Rosie in the letter how she felt about it and that she wasn't scared to leave when the time came.

But now at least she had proof that image was now her own for keeps, forever!

Rosie took a deep breath and folded the letter placing it in her jacket pocket and zipping it up tight.

"Right then Mils, we had better get to the Trugg's to help out. We'll keep these treats for Image…"

Millie enquired nosily, "Well, what was in the letter?"

"It was to grant me ownership of Image if anyone tries to say Image is theirs, also she is leaving me her mare and carriage when she dies as she's very ill, Mils," said Rosie quietly, fiddling with the charm bracelet she now wore on her wrist.

"I'm so sorry she's going to die, Rosie. I know you really liked her, she's made all your dreams come true giving you a pony, but she has given you her stuff for a reason. She obviously knows you are genuine and kind or she wouldn't have." Millie threw her arms around Rosie and gave her a big hug.

"Thank you, Mils, you are a good friend to me, you really are. Maybe when we are grown-ups we will live in the carriage traveling the countryside and we can learn about magical things as we travel along. We could even turn Emma and Flick into a pair of frogs!"

The girls laughed and started to head for the Trugg's farm as they had stables to muck out and horses to help with.

"I can't wait until later," said Millie.

"Me neither," said Rosie, as she walked down the lane. "I'm missing Image already."

Chapter 8

Rosie and Millie arrived at the Trugg's farm. Nipper was waiting for them at the gate, pressing his nose against it and breathing through the holes to try and detect how far away they were.

The girls finally got to the gate and pushed it open ushering Nipper out of the way.

It had got quite late by now so Mrs Trugg had done the mucking out and was bathing Bella her grey mare. "Hello girls, you've missed nearly all the fun, but you can go and pick up the droppings from Goliath and Bruno's paddock if you like, then you can bring them in and help me tack up, as Mr Trugg and I are going for a hack in a while."

"Yes, Mrs Trugg we'd love to." the girls ran off grabbing the bucket and scoop to clear up the droppings and headed off to help with the chores.

When the girls finished their chores, they grabbed the huge head collars, went to the field and brought the two giant horses in, they then tied them up ready to be groomed. Mrs Trugg approached the girls with a grooming box and said, "Well girls, you are doing a wonderful job of keeping my place tidy. I have a surprise for you. When your mum popped down, she and I had a little talk. She thought it was time for you to be allowed to ride."

Rosie felt a sudden pang of guilt knowing she had Image hidden and she should have asked her permission to have him.

Rosie smiled and said, "Mrs Trugg, I need to tell you something… but you have to keep this a secret for the moment." Rosie simply hated to lie and knew it would be impossible to keep this from the adults.

"Oh gosh, what is it, Rosie? What have you done? Why don't we go inside and I'll make us all a nice warm drink and let's see if we can sort this out, ok? I'm sure it's nothing that can't be sorted out children, come on," said Mrs Trugg, ushering the guilty looking girls into her warm kitchen.

They pulled up chairs and took a slurpy swig of the warm milk Mrs Trugg put down before them. Tears came to Rosie's eyes and she blurted out.

"This old gypsy woman gave me a pony and it lives in the woods because it has no coat pigment, I can't tell my parents as we can't afford a pony and you're probably selling the woodland, so he's going to have no home. I don't know what to do," she carried on sobbing.

Millie sat there a tear in her eye but still stuffing the homemade biscuits into her mouth so she couldn't speak even if she wanted to.

"Oh Rosie, you poor girl, this is a turn up for the

books, you having a hidden pony!" said Mrs Trugg, screwing up her face in wonder.

Rosie then had another outburst. "That's not all," pulling out the letter from her pocket and shoving it into Mrs Trugg's hands. "Mariella, the old gypsy woman, is very ill and when the time comes, she said she wants me to have her other horse and carriage, but I've nowhere to keep the other horse or the carriage.

I'd love to have them so much, but we only have a tiny cottage, we don't even have a driveway. Whatever will I do?"

Mrs Trugg pursed her lips and said, hmmm, to herself.

"Well girls, there's only one thing for it. Mr Trugg and I do not want to sell our farm as you know, but we are being forced by that awful, mean Digby Fox who is councillor for the area, he wants to build new houses where the ancient woodland is. We need to think of a way to stop him and save the woodland.

"But to do this, we need a very special reason indeed. If you girls can think of a way, it means that farmer Trugg and I can carry on running the farm and when the time comes, I don't see why you can't keep the two ponies here. I'm sure old Pip wouldn't mind the company.

"I'm not making you any promises though, as we have to stop the councilor from digging up the wood first and forcing us to sell the farm, not to mention the fact that you are going to have to be honest with your mum.

"She loves you very much and has always said she'd love to let you have a pony but she couldn't afford one.

"I believe half of your dreams have come true here. You have one pony, possibly another when your poor friend passes away, you and Millie will be able to ride together. Maybe I'll have a word with your mum first as I'm sure she will understand.

"Sometimes things are never as bad as they seem if you just talk them through" added Mrs Trugg,

"Thank you so much," cried Rosie, giving Mrs Trugg a huge smile.

"That's alright, dear, life is complicated sometimes, but everything will work itself out, just have a bit of faith."

The two girls smiled at each other and held hands over the table in relief that someone might be able to help them.

"Right then," said Mrs Trugg "you definitely need to learn to ride then, so come on, let's go and tack up and I'll show you the basics."

The girls dried their eyes, both ran up to Mrs Trugg and gave her a big kiss on each cheek, then ran outside to help prepare the horses.

Once the horses were groomed and had their hooves picked out the girls went into the old tack room.

There were so many old saddles and bridles from when the Trugg's children once had ponies and the tack remained. Rosie wondered to herself if one of the bridles would fit Image, she thought she had better learn how to tack up and ride before asking if she could borrow one.

The two girls lifted the heavy leather saddles and took them to where Goliath and Bruno were tied up, only just lifting them high enough to place them over the stable doors.

"Right girls, put the bridles on the hooks while I show you how to put the saddles on first. Now make sure you always sit the saddle forward, just behind the wither. Never push it forward towards the mane, always go in the direction of the pony's coat hair. Pull out any trapped mane so as to make the horse comfy, then take the girth and lower it, don't drop it in case it bashes your horse's legs.

"Then walk to the other side, lift your saddle flap and haul up your girth until it's tight enough to be able to mount.

"You don't want to be riding upside down now girls, do you?" she said giggling.

After the saddles were on properly, both girls grabbed a bridle. "Now hold the bridle in your right hand and loop your arm under the horse's chin so your arm and the bridle is then resting on the bridge of the horse's nose, with your left hand position the bit by the horse's lips and open the horse's mouth slightly to pop the bit in.

Then you can slide the bridle up and over the ears, do

up the bridle buckles on the nose-band and throat lash and that's it, you're all done," smiled Mrs Trugg.

Luckily Mrs Trugg's horses were very well behaved so the lesson was an easy one for the girls.

"Right, now we are all tacked up we can go for a little ride." Mrs Trugg attached lead ropes to the horse's bridles while the girls ran into the tack room to find riding hats that fitted them. "Right then, foot into the stirrups and up you get," said Mrs Trugg, positioning their feet correctly into the huge metal stirrups.

The horses were so big the girls only just managed to haul themselves into the saddles, but they felt safe even though the horses were huge, as they were quite quiet and well trained, plus Mrs Trugg was leading them.

Even though it was just a short walk around the farm it was a dream come true for them. Rosie was glad that she had the chance to ride before she tried to ride her pony, as she didn't want to get it wrong and hurt him by being clumsy with her arms and legs.

It was getting close to teatime and the girls had to go to their homes for tea. Mrs Trugg and Rosie walked Millie home, then Mrs Trugg accompanied Rosie as they had to have a little talk with Rosie's mum when they arrived.

Rosie took off her Jodhpur boots and went to wash while Mrs Trugg had a little chat with her mother.

Rosie thought it best to let the grown-ups talk, as she knew Mrs Trugg would try and talk her into thinking a new pony could only ever be a good thing because Mrs Trugg just loved all animals and especially horses and ponies.

After about thirty of the longest minutes in Rosie's life, her mum called her to the kitchen.

"Well, Rosie, you really should have asked me if it was ok to have a pony, let alone the possibility of being left with two. These creatures cost money to keep and they need land where they can eat and run around.

I'm not angry, I'm more upset you felt I wouldn't understand. Mrs Trugg has told me about your progress and says not only do you know the basics of riding, but you have kept her yard tidy for a long time now, so with that in mind you do seem responsible enough to keep a pony.

"I understand you own this pony now anyway so that's that, you are lucky I am superstitious as you know the old saying... never look a gift horse in the mouth!

"Now, Mrs Trugg has very kindly said you can use the old barn where her children used to keep their ponies before they left home. It's going to take you and Millie all week to get it straight, so I want you to promise to be good and do everything Mrs Trugg says.

And on a serious note, both of you girls must understand that the council may force the Truggs to sell the farm and then we really won't be able to keep the pony, but we'll worry about that later and of course, telling your father when he gets back from helping the vicar with mowing the church-yard.

I'll make him a nice meal to try and soften the blow, in the meantime madam, I want a sincere apology and you must thank Mrs Trugg very much for agreeing to help by putting herself out so much for you." Said Mrs Buckle

"Aw, it's no trouble, she's a good girl and she means well and any child who likes animals should be nurtured," said Mrs Trugg in a kind voice, winking at Rosie.

Mrs Buckle hummed and said, "Well nevertheless, her father is going to be a bit less understanding, but I'm sure he'll see the benefits of her having a pony." Rosie couldn't believe how smoothly everything had gone, she didn't receive half the telling off she thought she was going to get, but then she did genuinely feel bad about keeping this from her mother and father.

"Right then, madam, are you going to show us this pony then, as I had better take him back to the farm, the woods at night are no place for a little pony on his own now are they?" said Mrs Trugg.

Rosie nodded and grabbed the apple and carrot bits she had stored all day in her coat pocket.

"Come on, I'll call him. Come with me." Rosie grabbed some rope from the hook in the hallway and ran out of the house, through the front gate and up the woodland lane to the rear of their little cottage, she stood at the opening of the pathway into the woods, shut her eyes and in her head she called, 'Image, Image, Image'.

About twenty seconds later she heard hoof beats in the distance and saw a flicker of bright white appear through the dark trees. It was the most beautiful sight she had ever seen. She stood there, her heart beating like a drum at the realisation her adventure of the night before was not a dream. It was real and galloping to her calls.

As the creature grew ever closer, Rosie could see him showing off an extended trot with his neck arched and his horn pointing out in front.

"Hello Rosie, my friend," he called out, smiling at the little girl.

"Hello Image, I really missed you. Are you alright?" she said to the beautiful unicorn now standing in front of her.

"I had to tell the grown-ups you were my pony, otherwise things would have become very difficult. The kind farmer's wife is going to let you live in the barn.

Millie and I are going to make it really nice for you, at some point, your mum may be coming to live with you."

Rosie looked sad.

"Mariella is unwell?" asked the unicorn.

"Sadly she is very ill, but has said I am going to look after your mother and the carriage that she lives in when the time comes," said Rosie.

The unicorn paused and replied, "It is sad but when our time is spent on the earth we must all go back to Unus for him to breathe a new life back into us."

Rosie nodded as it would take her some time to come to terms with this, but she understood.

She looked around and Mrs Trugg and her mother were walking up the lane towards her and her unicorn. The unicorn took a step back unsure of the approaching strangers.

"It's alright, Mrs Trugg is going to look after you, I will visit you tomorrow and start clearing out the barn to make you a new home," Rosie assured Image.

"Well alright, if you say they are our friends I believe

you."

The unicorn licked Rosie's face and put his head on her shoulder.

"Oh! What a beautiful pony," said Mrs Buckle.

Mrs Trugg agreed that he was a really showy type, fine but strong with good bones. Neither of the adults could see his horn, to them, he was just a very pretty pony. When he spoke all that came to their ears was a neigh.

But Rosie understood every word he said. "See you tomorrow, Image," said Rosie, and kissed his velvety pink muzzle.

"See you too, Rosie," said Image.

"He neighs a lot, doesn't he?" said Mrs Trugg laughing. "Let me take that bag of treats to make him up a delicious feed for his supper and I'll see you in the morning for mucking out duty," she added.

Then Rosie replied, "Thank you so much again for everything Mrs Trugg, I'll see you tomorrow bright and early."

Chapter 9

Morning couldn't come soon enough for Rosie, the sun was barely up and she was jumping out of bed.

She could hear her mother stirring and calling in a sleepy tone, "You're not going out without breakfast, madam, so wait up, let me come and make it now."

Oh, thought Rosie, I want to see Image right now!

She went downstairs and raided the vegetable rack for Carrots, chopped them up into bite sized pieces whilst she waited for her mother to come down and make breakfast.

Her mother rolled into the kitchen, her hair standing up on end and said, "Rosie-May, I know you're excited, but this is early, even for you!"

Rosie smiled the widest smile, humming a happy tune, tipping all the chopped carrots into a bag. "Oh, Mum, I'm so excited. A real pony of my very own, can we go to the tack shop today and buy a new head collar please? I'll buy it from my savings if that is ok, Mum?" she pleaded.

"Well I suppose he'll need a nice head collar. Oh, alright, I'll come and pick you up at about ten thirty once you have cleaned his stable and done lots of chores for

Mrs Trugg. You make sure you help her with whatever needs doing as all this is very good of her you know."

Rosie smiled and said, "I know, Mrs Trugg is the nicest woman I've ever met, she's always teaching me about the horses. I think maybe I will grow up and work with horses, don't you, Mum?"

Mrs Buckle rolled her eyes, smiled to herself and said, "I think it's more than likely Rosie, I really do. Right, madam, eat your scrambled eggs on toast and drink this orange juice my love, then you can go and see your pony."

Rosie bolted the food down and nearly got indigestion as she just couldn't eat it fast enough. She drank back the orange juice and kissed her mum on the cheek smearing her with butter, crumbs and orange juice.

"Thank you, Rosie, see you later," said her mother, shaking her head.

Rosie arrived at the Trugg's. Farmer Trugg was loading some cattle into a trailer. "Morning Rosie, I'm just off to market so I'll see you later."

Nipper was running around farmer Trugg in frantic circles and then jumped into the back of his old green Land Rover.

Rosie wandered down to the stables where Mrs Trugg was turning out Goliath and Bruno.

She fed Bella and Pip inside, to stop them being bullied by the bigger horses.

"I've made you up a feed for your pony my dear, he's in the end stable as he can't go in the barn until we've cleared it properly, alright?"

"If it gets sunny we can just pull the top door across, he'll be alright, what do they call these ponies? Albinos?" asked Rosie curiously.

"No, you can't get true Albino horses, you get something called a double dilute cream or a cremello. They have beautiful pink skin and fine white or creamy hairs, their eyes are like glass blue, they are very rare and it is said they have magic powers, but that's all fairy stories," laughed Mrs Trugg.

Image then stuck his head over the door and said to Rosie, "Ha-ha well, that's what she thinks! We are unicorns! That's If we are summoned of course, we can't all be picked as we have to inherit a horn from the previous unicorn, she's right about our skin though, if I stay out in strong sunlight it will hurt my skin, I find the light very bright in my eyes, but at night I can see perfectly."

"Fantastic, well, now I know," said Rosie.

"That's alright, my dear, I'm here to help you." Said Mrs Trugg, not realising Rosie was actually speaking to Image!

"Enough of this talking, can I have my breakfast please, Rosie? I'm starving. The hay was alright I suppose, but I much prefer carrots, oh that food in the bucket she gave me last night was yummy," said the hungry unicorn, pawing at the ground and licking his lips.

"Ok boy, here's your breakfast," said Rosie, going into the stable and tipping the mixture into his manger.

"Mmm yum yum mmm," she heard coming from the manger as the little unicorn chomped his way through his breakfast hardly lifting his head up for air.

Rosie mucked out, then helped skip out the field.

Ten thirty came around quickly and Rosie said to Mrs Trugg, "I'm just popping to the tack shop to buy a new head collar for Image. I'll be back just after lunch to start on the barn. Is it still alright for Millie to come and join me, as it'll be easier with the two of us. Oh and do you need anything from the tack shop?" asked Rosie.

"Of course, that's fine and yes, could you get me a chalk block and a tail bandage for Bella please," said Mrs Trugg.

Rosie smiled and said, "Of course. I'll see you later."

Rosie went up to the gate where her mum was already waiting for her, they all exchanged waves, then Rosie and her mum headed off to the next village where Mindy's tack shop was.

Rosie loved it in there, but before now, she never had a pony of her own to buy anything for.

Although she would occasionally pop in to buy something for Mrs Trugg and see all the other girls with their ponies outside, Rosie was just dreaming of the day when she would have a pony of her own.

That day had come, she thought, only now I have something very special that is just for me to see. In her mind she could see Image galloping towards her looking fantastic, while all the children that had ignored her before as she had no pony, stood aside as the most beautiful pony they ever saw rode by with Rosie on top smiling.

Oh what a dream, thought Rosie, it'll be real soon.

Rosie smiled to herself as she walked past all the girls with their little brown and bay ponies.

She did, of course, love all ponies but she knew even if Image had just been a normal pony he would still have been the most beautiful pony in the world.

Rosie and her mum went into Mindy's and saw the rows of pretty coloured matching tack.

"Do you want pink?" asked Rosie's mum.

"Pink!? No way, he's a boy I can't make him wear pink. I'm going to get black, which will make him stand out and look beautiful," smiled Rosie, picking out a beautiful black leather head collar with a brass plaque to have the pony's name printed on.

Perfect she thought, as she grabbed Mrs Trugg's items and went to the checkout. Mrs Buckle placed a black hoof pick, a real bristle body brush, a dandy brush, a curry comb and a sweat rug on the counter and said, "Right, we'll have these as well."

"Oh thank you so much, Mum. This is just the best day's shopping ever!" beamed Rosie.

Mindy turned to Rosie and said, "Oh, you have more than five items so you can have either a grooming box or a new hat silk for free."

Rosie couldn't believe her luck and chose her free gift.

"May I have that black grooming box please, Mindy?" smiled Rosie.

"Of course you can, tell you what, seeing as you're so polite, here's some mint horse treats as well for your pony," said Mindy.

"Oh thanks Mrs Mindy," said Rosie, waving the freebies at her mum and smiling.

Mindy smiled at Rosie and said, "No probs sweetheart, the other girls are so rude it doesn't make you want to give them free bits and bobs, so I don't! Anyway, I think it looks like someone has a new pony, am I right?"

Rosie grinned. "I do, yes, and he's the best pony in the whole world!" Inside, Rosie knew he was more than special and more than just a normal pony! She knew she had to keep quiet about his magic secret.

Mrs Buckle then piped up, "He's a real beauty, isn't he, Rosie-May?"

Mindy leant over the counter and said, "Do bring him down sometime, I'd love to see him when he's settled and you're riding out, I'd love to meet him."

"I will definitely ride to the shop to show you him," said Rosie, happy at the thought of riding out and showing off her unicorn!

The two left the shop all smiles, pushing their way past the girls outside the shop. Rosie could see from the corner of her eye one of the girls on a little brown grumpy looking pony with a star. She didn't realize it was Emma at first as she looked different with her skull cap on.

Just wait until you see my pony, thought Rosie, I bet

that Flick and Emma will try and make friends, no way thought Rosie, not after how mean they have been to Mils, especially Emma.

Rosie and her mum walked up to Mr Lovett's shop.

"Oh two seconds Mum, can I just grab my pony mag whilst we are here?"

"Yes that makes sense Rosie, you pop on in," nodded her mother. Rosie pushed open the heavy door and Mr Lovett came waltzing out from the rear of the shop.

"Well hello Rosie-May, so how did it go? From the looks of all your Mindy bags the magic spell worked, all you have to say yes or no? Tell me, tell me?" asked Mr Lovett excitedly.

"It worked, Mr Lovett, he's the most fantastic creature you could ever see. I will ride him down here when it isn't sunny as he can't go out in the sunlight. You just have to meet him," said Rosie.

"That'd be fantastic. I'd be honoured to meet him," said Mr Lovett, with a quiver in his voice.

"Right then, I had better grab my pony mag or mum will be wondering where I've got to."

Mr Lovett also gave her a little selection of sweets in a bag, he said shoving a bag of sweets in to her hands. "You have made my day young lady, you deserve these and I won't take no for an answer, come back soon Rosie-May and take care."

Rosie and her mum then walked home, picking up Millie on the way through. They all had a nice ploughman's lunch at Rosie's house, then the two girls wandered over to farmer Trugg's to start clearing out the barn.

As they walked past the farmer he said, "Right then, a pile to go on the bonfire, the old hay and straw on the muck heap, give Mrs Trugg a call when it's completely clear as she'll have to help you disinfect the barn ready to put the clean bedding down, then you can move your pony in.

"Make up two stables in there as Pip can come in with him. It'll do her good to be in the warm this winter... if we're still here," said Mr Trugg, under his breath looking at the ground.

Rosie and Millie sat on a straw bale putting their heads together, there must be something we can do, there just must, maybe Image will know, thought Rosie. I'll have to ask him when Millie's not around so she doesn't think I've gone completely mad and I'm talking to myself.

After they wore themselves out clearing half of the barn, they decided to spend the rest of the time sitting with Image.

Rosie managed to have a half conversation with him as most pony owners talk to their ponies so it didn't seem too crazy to Millie.

He really enjoyed being groomed with his new brushes

they felt like a brilliant massage to Image. This is the life, he thought and then was rewarded with carrot bits and a kiss from both girls.

"I love you," said Image to Rosie, looking at her with big glass blue eyes,

"I love you Image, you are the most beautiful creature in the whole world." He leant his cheek on her, tickling her nose with his long silky white mane and smiled to himself at how happy he was to have found such a loving friend.

Chapter 10

Another day dawned and Rosie yawned a big smile, her mind full of her magic secret and her new best friend, Image. I wonder what we should do today, thought Rosie.

Her friend Millie couldn't come out every day because her parents were quite strict. From an early age, Rosie had been allowed to spend time at the Trugg's farm as Rosie's mum had gone to school with Mrs Trugg's eldest daughter and they were family friends.

This made it all the sadder in Rosie's mind that the Truggs would have to give up their beautiful home. Not without a fight, thought Rosie to herself.

I must be able to think of a way to help. She peered out of her bedroom window at the beautiful old trees, and she couldn't bear the thought of the trees being bulldozed and new houses being put in their place. What about all the little woodland creatures she thought, where will they go?

She looked up to the sky and saw that it was heavy and overcast. Hooray! she thought, this means I can take Image out without him being in danger.

"Dull days are fantastic for unicorns as their skin is safe from the sun's harmful rays." Rosie hopped out of bed and shuffled down to the bathroom, had a quick wash and changed into her jodhpurs, then shot down the stairs where her mum was standing with a bag of carrot peelings saying, "Not until you've eaten, madam!'

Rosie groaned in agreement and sat in her place at the table.

"You must eat so you're strong enough to look after that pony, Rosie-May."

Rosie perked up in agreement. "Yes you're right, Mum," she said finishing her breakfast. She grabbed the carrot peelings, ran out of the door and down the garden path. On the lane was a council van with boards saying NEW HOUSES EXPECTED AT EDENSBATCH. VILLAGE VOTE TAKING PLACE AT THE VILLAGE HALL IN ONE WEEK'S TIME AT 6PM. MP ATTENDING.

Great, thought Rosie, I have a week to think of a plan, I have to stop this, I simply have to. As she started walking down the street she could see two girls coming towards her.

Oh no, thought Rosie, it's Emma and Flick. As they approached her they stood over her.

Emma said, "Well, I hear you have a gypsy pony, can't afford a real one then? You've been hanging around with the witch for too long, that's why you have a gypsy pony and not a real pony, ha-ha," she said to Rosie, laughing a cruel laugh.

Emma piped up again, "It's probably a real old nag that they didn't want, anyway. Flicks dad's going to tear down that smelly old wood behind your house and make lots of money.

"He says if he builds these new houses she can have a show pony, a beautiful well bred show pony, not like your nag, oh and those farmers will be moved into one of the new houses, so you won't have anywhere to keep your pony... oh dear, what a shame," she spat in a mean voice.

Flick was quietly standing behind her. Rosie gritted her teeth as she knew that what Emma wanted was for her to start an argument, so she took a deep breath and said, "Well aren't you lucky, I'll have to hope I'm not in a show class next to you or in a race as I suppose I'll lose," and calmly walked by the two confused girls.

Emma expected Rosie to get angry at her comments, but Rosie knew she would have the last laugh as Image was no nag, he was no pony either...! Oh, just wait until they see me on him, she thought to herself smiling.

She arrived at the farm and did her chores for Mrs Trugg, then Mrs Trugg uttered the magic words, "Shall we go for a hack today? I can lead you on your new pony, if you like."

Mrs Trugg took for it granted that Image was broken in because he looked older and was very sensible to lead, after feeding him the carrot bits Rosie asked Image.

"Is it ok if I ride you? Only Mrs Trugg has offered to

lead me on you."

Image looked at her and laughed saying, "Lead me? I'm not crazy you know! I can remember how to be ridden from my last life... well, vaguely, anyway."

The unicorn arched his neck and started trotting on the spot. "Oh and another thing Image, there's two really horrid girls who called you a nag, if we bump into them could you do that neck arching thing and the trotting on the spot if they see us?" asked Rosie.

"Of course, it'd be my pleasure. horrid girls hey, we'll see about that then," said Image to Rosie. Rosie went on to explain to Image about all the nasty things they had said and done to Millie and how Flick's father was a corrupt councilor and was tearing down the wood.

He looked at Rosie with caring eyes nibbling at her jacket. "It'll be alright, we'll think of a plan and save the farm and the wood. I am here to protect you and do good deeds, remember?" Image assured her.

Rosie nodded reaching into her grooming box for a body brush and started to brush his silky white coat. "It's not as if we are causing trouble, we are saving the woodland and the Trugg's farm, it's ok to help those you love," said Rosie. She could hear Mrs Trugg tacking up Bella outside in the yard and thought she had better go and grab some tack for Image.

Rosie left Image happily eating some hay and went into the tack room. She picked out one of Mrs Trugg's children's pony's old saddles, they were all kept clean as Rosie and Mrs Trugg liked to clean tack together in the yard.

She took a little black saddle and bit-less bridle to where Image was and went in. "Oh tack, I remember! Thank you for choosing a bit-less bridle as metal bits taste nasty," said the unicorn, sniffing at the old saddle.

Rosie turned to Image and said, "I'm sorry I have to put tack on at all, but we don't want to arouse suspicion that you're not a normal pony, ok?"

"Hhhmmmm... ok," sighed the unicorn, snorting and stretching his legs. "I suppose I had better pretend to be a bit pony-like!" Rosie placed the saddle on his back and did up the girth very gently. "Oooh it tickles! Don't pull it too tight please, Rosie," he looked around at her.

"I won't, don't worry, it just needs to be tight enough so it doesn't slip." She then slipped the bridle on and led him out of the stable.

Mrs Trugg passed her a riding hat and held her stirrup, Rosie placed her foot in the stirrup and Image started moving about. "What are you doing?" Rosie whispered to Image.

The little Unicorn turned around and replied, "Well we have to make me seem like a normal pony, remember?" Rosie then grabbed the front of the saddle and hauled herself up.

It was like magic thought Rosie, being up here on my

very own unicorn. She felt like a princess in a rather cool horsey dream!

Mrs Trugg then mounted a rather impatient Bella and they set off clopping up the cobbles in the farmyard. Farmer Trugg opened the gate and let them both through and they set off towards the next village. Across open fields they trotted and cantered, the wind in Image's mane and tail.

Mrs Trugg kept looking at him to look at his obvious beauty. "He's a smashing pony you know Rosie. You are the luckiest girl, your friends are going to envy you so much."

Rosie smiled and stroked Image's neck, fiddling with strands of his mane. "That tickles," said Image.

"Sorry," whispered Rosie, leaning forward to speak in his ear.

They came to the next village where the shops were and best of all Mindy's tack shop was.

Rosie could see some of the girls who usually hung out there on their ponies, they rode past a couple of them and they actually went past and saw the girls mouths open in shock at Rosie's beautiful pony. "There you go Rosie, proof that he's a stunner," said Mrs Trugg, as they approached Mindy's tack shop.

The moment she had been waiting for had come at last. Out walked Flick and Emma. At first they didn't think it was Rosie, you could see that in their faces, but as Rosie and Mrs Trugg grew closer to them they noticed her on the stunning pony. Flick actually dropped her bag of goodies from Mindy's.

"Quick Image, that's them," said Rosie in his ear. Image then started to do a Spanish walk and then trotted on the spot with his tail held high in the air and his neck arched, his flowing long white mane and tail trailing behind almost lashing Flick and Emma across their shocked faces.

Rosie could hear Flick saying, "Oh my gosh, how the hoof oil did she get that pony? It's amazing!"

Emma then shushed Flick and both girls looked at each other, their faces bitterly screwed up as if they had just shared a horse fly flavoured sandwich, then they stormed off looking extremely jealous indeed.

"That showed them! Can I stop trotting on the spot now please, I'm tired of pretending to do the Spanish walk thing, it makes my legs ache, you know."

Image stopped and did a big shake, rattling Rosie and making her giggle. Mrs Trugg looked at Rosie and said, "It's as if he knew how to make those girls jealous... how clever! I wish my horses were that clever."

Ah, thought Rosie, but this is no pony, he's a unicorn. How I wish Millie could have been with me to see what happened, she would have loved to see the look on their faces!

After Mrs Trugg picked up her order from Mindy's they hacked home across the fields, taking the long route through the woods as you could cut through to the glade and jump a fallen tree that was in the middle.

Bella and Image galloped smoothly together through the trees. Image going slowly so as not to wear Bella out, as unicorns are faster than any other horses, they are also great jumpers as Rosie found out flying across the log.

Mrs Trugg shouted out, "That's amazing. I was going to tell you to wait while I jumped it, I thought you couldn't ride!"

"Oh I've read a lot of books on how to do it Mrs Trugg," said Rosie smiling, trying to sound convincing, as it's common knowledge that when you ride a unicorn it's like being balanced on a soft beanbag. They are so comfy and smooth you barely know you are riding at all.

But then Mrs Trugg had no clue Image was a unicorn, to her he was just a very very special pony.

Chapter 11

It was like a dream week, as if the weather had been arranged especially for Rosie and Image, they rode out every single day.

Rosie's riding skills got much better, even though unicorns were very simple to ride she still gained riding knowledge.

Millie came to the farm several times and helped groom. She never asked to mount Image, as really Millie was a little nervous of riding anything too fast. Being lead by Mrs Trugg was one thing, but riding out alone was another.

The pony would have to be very ploddy for Millie to feel safe, so she enjoyed cycling alongside Rosie and Image.

She had a basket on the front of her bike so she brought little picnic lunches and carrots for Image, when they stopped for rests.

Sooner or later the time came when they bumped into Emma and Flick again. Flick stood back and let Emma do the talking. As usual, Emma started on Millie.

"Oh no," said Millie, "leave me alone."

Emma mimicked Millie, "Oh please leave me alone. What a baby, hey Flick? Wah wah wah."

With that, Image put his head down, pointing his horn at Emma's mouth. "I think it's time to teach this one a lesson," said Image.

Then, as if literally by magic, every word that came out of Emma's mouth was wah wah wah, just like the sound of a real crying baby!

She put her hand over her mouth and pulled her lips about to try and fix her speech, she ran off with Flick in tow and all you could hear was wah wah going off into the distance.

Rosie and Millie started to laugh huge belly laughs. "What on earth happened?" asked Millie.

Rosie looked at Image and he said, "Well my trick for nasty people is… what you say is what you are, so she'll be a baby for an hour or so then it'll wear off and she'll be able to speak again."

All Millie could hear were Image's neighs.

Rosie said to Millie, "Search me?" Laughing at the clever little unicorn's trick, which was great, both the girls agreed, then they all set off for the Trugg's again.

Suddenly, Flick appeared once more running over to the two girls and Image, she surprised both Millie and Rosie and said, "Look I'm sorry I've been horrible Millie, but I just went along with Emma as I thought she was my friend, but she is being really weird and making baby noises.

I tried to ask her if I could help and she kicked me in the shins and slammed her front door in my face. Friends don't do that. You two are so lucky to have each other.

I now realise that Emma was only hanging out with me to use me and because she thinks I'm getting a new pony.

I do want a pony, but it's not fair you should lose yours just so my step dad can make his money with these new houses. He only wants to buy me a pony to keep me quiet, anyway he pushes me and mum around you see, he's not a nice man at all.

In fact he's cruel and when I go home he makes me go to my room and stay there every single day. Please accept my apology both of you, especially Millie as I've been so awful to you," said Flick, begging for forgiveness.

Rosie and Millie looked at each other and agreed it was best to forgive her because she had been sucked in by Emma's false friendship and been turned into a bully. "Ok Flick, but one mean comment and that's it, we won't give you another chance," said Rosie.

"I forgive you," said Millie.

Flick then said, "There must be some way I can make it up to you both, can I help clean the stables or your tack? Only dad mustn't see I'm at the Trugg's or I'll be in real trouble, he's trying to get the land from your farmer friend you see.

If only there was a way I could help you as I know my step dad Digby's up to no good. If there was a way we could prove it, maybe the police would take him away and lock him in a prison.

Then mum and I could live in peace without being shouted at all of the time by Digby."

Image piped up. "Ask her to find proof and give it to you, we have just twenty-four hours before that meeting about the woods being bulldozed.

She could help us and then we could help her. We could scupper his plans, don't worry I will cast a truth spell on the evil Mr Digby Fox. He won't have a choice but to say exactly what he's up to!" smiled Image at Rosie.

Rosie explained Image's ideas to Flick as if it were her own and Flick promised to try and find some proof and meet up with them the next day outside the back of the village hall where the meeting was to be held. She went off waving goodbye.

Rosie and Millie agreed she had meant what she'd said, but tomorrow would be the proof.

Millie said, "How awful of her nasty step-father making her stay in her room and being terrible to her mum, no wonder she hung around with Emma, it must have made her feel safer I suppose."

"I am glad we are all friends as I don't like not getting along with people," Rosie agreed.

Image nodded and put his head on Millie. "Aw, you are a lovely pony," said Millie.

"I know," said Image. "I know." And they went back to the Trugg's.

They settled Image in his stable with a nice big feed leaving him munching happily with his head in his manger. They then went to the barn where they had nearly finished making it nice again as they did a little every day and had found some old paint and started to paint the stalls again.

They had an hour before they had to be home, so they finished off their painting and bedded the two stables down for Pip and Image.

Farmer Trugg walked in and saw what the girls had done to the barn and the girls saw sadness in his eyes. "Oh Farmer Trugg, it'll be ok, you'll see, you won't have to sell the farm," said Rosie, putting her hand on Farmer Trugg's shoulder and patting it.

"Aw you're a sweet girl, but tomorrow will tell my dear, tomorrow will tell. In that meeting in the town hall everyone will be taking a vote whether the council will force me to sell my land and home. That Digby Fox has a good case, he knows all the city jargon so what chance do we have? We are just country folk, my dear," said Farmer Trugg, looking at the girls sadly.

"There's always hope, Farmer Trugg," said Millie, looking at the old farmer.

"There is child, there is," said Farmer Trugg unconvincingly as he wandered out of the barn. Nipper following at his heels.

The two girls looked at each other and held up their crossed fingers at each other, but Rosie knew something Millie and indeed no-one else did, even if Flick didn't come up trumps with any evidence, Image was going to cast a spell, a Unicorn magic truth spell!

Rosie and Millie finished tidying up the paint pots and swept the indoor stables to perfection. It looked fantastic, four little indoor stables with two large open stalls opposite them, a room for hay at the end and a little room next to it.

Rosie assumed the children used to keep all their tack and grooming kit in it as there were old dusty saddle racks along the wall and some cobwebby old lead ropes where the head collars must have hung up.

"Maybe if all goes to plan we can ask if we can make this our own private tack room Rosie," said Millie.

"Yes, that'd be nice, Mils, we could make it all clean and tidy and make a board where we could stick photos and hopefully, one day, rosettes. Let's hope all goes well and we get to keep all our hard work, hey Millie?" said Rosie.

"Yes I'm sure Flick will try and help us, you'll see," nodded Millie.

The two girls shut the barn door. Mrs Trugg was just

putting the ducks and chickens away to bed in their coups in the yard.

"Millie you go on home, I'm going to spend ten minutes with Image before I go."

She waved Millie off and went into Image's stable, where he was lying down and nodding off to sleep in the cosy bed Rosie had made for him.

"Hi Rosie, I was just having forty winks. I need to get lots of sleep tonight if I am to summon a brilliant spell on that horrid man tomorrow, the more evil the person, the harder the spell is to make, as it takes up a lot of my magic power and I'll have to rest for ages to regain it again afterwards you know," said the little unicorn laying his head on Rosie's lap and looking at her with his big blue eyes.

Rosie looked at her little unicorn and said, "Image, this really is important you know? We could lose this place if we can't come up with something."

Image sat up and pushed Rosie's hair out of her eyes with his pink velvet muzzle. "Look, young lady, you listen to me, it's all going to be fine because evil people are their own undoing, you know.

"Unus sees to that, he has a plan for every single one of us, I'm just glad I'm here on earth with such a kind friend like you, so keep your chin up, we can do this and save the ancient woodland and when we do, we can explore it together," assured Image.

"What about all those stories people say about the paths changing?" said Rosie.

"I'm sure whatever we find, we can overcome together, Rosie it's you and me kiddo, remember?" said Image, winking at Rosie.

Yes, thought Rosie, you and me. She gave the little unicorn a kiss on the cheek and then shut his stable doors so that he could sleep well. Setting off for home, she shut the Trugg's gate and glanced across the yard. In the distance the Trugg's stood with their arms around one another just rocking each other. Poor Truggs, gulped Rosie and took a slow thoughtful walk home.

Chapter 12

The day of reckoning dawned. Rosie peered out of her bedroom window at the wood behind her house, beautiful in its gloomy darkness with a mist hovering around it like a floating quilt nestling up to the trunks. Rosie sighed at the reality of it being ploughed up and houses being stuck in its place. It didn't seem possible that humans could do this to such a beautiful place, didn't they care about trees or the animals that lived in the woodland for generations? Rosie sniffed and then got herself ready for breakfast.

"Good morning Rosie, not a cheerful day for the Truggs hey? That blooming meeting, it's no place for children you know, you really shouldn't turn up there as there may be a lot of shouting when..." Mrs Buckle paused. "...if the council's plans go their way and they win," she finished.

Rosie stared at her scrambled eggs on toast as if it were invisible and then said, "There's always hope, Mum. We must be positive for the Trugg's sake." She could feel her heart sink at the thought of losing the place where she kept Image.

Mrs Buckle raised her eyebrows and they both just sat there in silence. Apart from the crunching of toast and occasional slurp of orange juice, breakfast seemed to go on for hours.

It was the first time Rosie and her mum didn't talk at breakfast. "Right I'm off to muck out and groom Image," said Rosie.

"Ah ok, there's a bag of chopped apple on the side for you, sweetheart," said Mrs Buckle, sniffing quietly as she was secretly scared her daughter would have to give up her one love… Image.

Rosie arrived at the farm and there was a very tense atmosphere.

Mrs Trugg walked up to Rosie and said, "Don't worry, it's just that Digby Fox has been here, he's saying we won't possibly win this and don't bother to go to the meeting. He also said when he wins and we have to sell, he will give you two hundred pounds for Image to give to his daughter."

Rosie started to panic, thoughts raced through her mind. What if Flick had tricked her and this was all a horrid plan to get Image for herself? Oh my goodness, thought Rosie.

She rushed in to see Image, who was just stirring. Rosie started gabbling but Image yawned and said, "Whoa, slow down I can't understand you when you speak that quickly. Slow down and tell me what the matter is, Rosie."

Rosie shuffled around nervously. "It's Flick, I think

she has tricked us, maybe she hasn't got any proof after all, what are we going to do if you can't get to Digby to cast the magic spell on him?" cried Rosie.

The unicorn hummed and aahed and then said, "Is there a window in the town hall?"

Rosie replied, "Yes they are all the way down the side of the building."

"Right then, when we get there, I will wait around the back where Flick is supposed to meet you. You go in and open the window by the front as I just need to get a clear aim with my horn so I can cast the spell, so keep calm, it'll be ok," smiled Image.

Rosie calmed down a little and put a head collar on Image. Millie turned up and offered to do Rosie's chores while Rosie groomed Image.

To Rosie, this maybe the last time she got to do this, especially if Flick had tricked them and Image couldn't cast a spell. It was all just too awful to think of. She stood with her arms around the little unicorn holding him tightly and praying for the right thing to happen.

Meanwhile at the Fox's home, Flick's step-father, Digby, had caught Flick with some of his private paperwork that would land him in real trouble.

He started shouting loudly at the little girl and it frightened her. He then turned to her mother who was telling Flick to go to her room before Digby got really cross.

While his back was turned, she had managed to grab one piece of important paperwork and stuff it into her pocket. Digby turned and started shouting at Flick again, while her mother tried to pull Digby away, so he grabbed her by the arm and shoved her into the pantry locking the door with her in there.

He then turned to Flick and marched her to her bedroom and locked her in. He removed the key shouting loudly through the door at her, "And you're both staying locked up in this house until I win this today. A little brat like you isn't going to stop my plans!" and then stormed out of the house, slamming the front door behind him.

Flick ran to her window and saw him walking off into the distance. All this made Flick even more sure she had to get rid of her evil step-father, she may have been promised a pony, but she had to stop him being so mean, shouting at her and her mother, who deserved better.

Bravely the little girl opened her bedroom window. She grabbed her sheets and tied them to her bed frame so she could lower herself to where she could jump down to the garden. She climbed out on the ledge and slid down the sheet holding on tight so as not to fall. When she lowered herself enough, she jumped spraining her ankle, but she hobbled around to the back door and let her poor mother out of the pantry.

Then she remembered she had to get to the village hall. She pulled on a hooded top so she wouldn't be recognised and set off hobbling as fast as she could up the road.

At the other end, Rosie and Millie were waiting behind the village hall with Image. "It's no good Millie, I'm going to have to go in, you stay and watch Image for me."

She wandered through the gathering crowds. There were hundreds of people and some protestors trying to save the woodland that were standing with placards with writing on at the door of the village hall.

She pushed her way in and gasped. The hall was full of people from front to back, all the seats were taken and people lined the walls. Oh no! thought Rosie, I must get to the window at the front, I simply must.

She squeezed through gaps in between people all the way to the front noticing that the very front windows were actually behind a barrier for the councilors to sit behind.

That's it! thought Rosie, she bent down getting onto her hands and knees and crawled under the table barrier and stood up opposite the stage and quickly opened the window.

An usher approached. "Good idea, child, but you need to go back to the other side, this is the councilors' side, go on, off you go," said the usher.

But it was ok, because Rosie had managed to open the window right opposite where Digby would be. She crawled back under the table and found a spot to hide where she could see and then waited.

Bang Bang Bang went the hammer to get everyone's attention in the hall. The councilors and an important looking man in a smart suit walked in and they all sat down at the front facing the crowd.

Rosie heard people murmuring that's the MP, she didn't know what an MP was, but she knew he must be important.

As the meeting went on people stood up and gave their views and the councilors, one by one they made their speech on whether they thought the wood should be bulldozed or not so that houses could be built.

Then Digby stood up. Rosie saw Image's nose come through the window. He pointed his magic Unicorn horn at Digby Fox and all of a sudden the strangest thing happened.

As if Digby had no control of what he was saying he explained to the whole hall and shocked councilors, including the MP, how he'd forged fake documents so that farmer Trugg would have to sell the farm.

With that he started laughing uncontrollably. His face grew redder and redder where he was trying so hard not to speak as every word he uttered was the truth, but the harder he tried, the faster the words came out of his mouth!

Outside Flick had got to Millie and Image and explained what had happened. Poor Flick, they thought, as she pulled out the crumpled piece of paper and said smiling, "Here's enough proof to lock him away for a long time."

With that, the little unicorn snatched it from her with his teeth and went to the front of the hall where the policemen were all standing.

Image pushed the note into a policeman's hand. He read the piece of crumpled paper, then showing his fellow policemen they all charged into the hall grabbing the evil Councilor Fox, who was still laughing uncontrollably under the Unicorn's magic truth spell.

They dragged Digby out kicking and screaming, still red faced and shouting the truth. As they started pulling him from the hall, roars of laughter filled the packed hall as the villagers had never seen such a bizarre show.

The MP stood up and banged the hammer to call attention once again and said, "Just to say, your village woodland is safe. There will be no bulldozers here at Edensbatch not now or ever." He smiled and left the stage to a very loud cheer from all of the village folk. People were jumping up and down, hugging each other and saying thank goodness.

After a while the crowd calmed and they started to leave for home. Rosie followed the crowd out of the hall and caught up with Image and Millie.

Flick was there and she explained to Rosie what had happened. Then she went off and told the policeman what else the evil Digby had done that day, the policeman put his hand on her little shoulder and said, "Don't worry he won't be leaving police custody in a hurry, that's for sure."

Rosie looked around at all of the happy faces in the crowd, the whole village was overjoyed that they got to keep the old woodland.

Through the crowd, Farmer Trugg and his wife pushed their way out and ran over to Rosie with big beaming smiles.

"Rosie! Millie! Have you heard? It's all going to be alright after all, you were right Rosie-May, we won the case! We won!"

"Digby went mad in there and it was the strangest thing, he owned up to everything he had done, it was amazing you should have been there."

Rosie smiled to herself as she and Image would only ever be the ones that really knew the truth of that day, the day they saved the wood and the day they secured their time together by saving the Trugg's farm. It would be their happy secret.

The people all started to head home. They all split off, Millie went home and Rosie jumped up onto Image's back and they headed off towards the wood.

Suddenly, Emma leapt out of the bushes in front of them and hissed, "Right, Miss Perfect Pony I don't know what happened the other day, but something's going on and I'm going to find out.

It's that evil frog-faced witch you hang around with, isn't it? You're all going to pay for making me look silly…"

With that Image, gave a big sigh and said to Rosie, "Here we go again," pointing his horn at Emma as she spat her poisonous words at them. With that her skin started to bubble and go a dark green colour, slime started to appear on her skin and she started to shrink, then she opened her mouth. Rosie expected her to speak but out popped a long frog tongue swatting a fly that was trying to land on Image. The unicorn laughed and said to Rosie, "I think that's a result! Maybe she'd like a job catching flies at the stable yard?"

Rosie and Image laughed so hard as they watched the angry Emma shrink down into a little green frog.

Image looked down and said, "You would think you'd have learned your lesson the first time little miss. As I said before, what you say is what you are." Emma was croaking furiously in what must have been angry frog language at the very amused Rosie and her unicorn friend. In the end she hopped off into the bushes.

Image looked at Rosie. "I think she's hopping mad! Don't worry, it'll wear off later when she calms down, maybe she'll think twice before being so horrid next time."

As they approached the entrance of the wood it looked deep and dark, as they stood there with the woodland mist circling Image's fetlocks, Rosie said to her Unicorn, "Should I be scared, Image?"

Image gazed at her with his crystal clear blue eyes and said, "You never need to be scared when I'm with you, Rosie, not ever."

He pointed his horn into the woodland opening. "We don't know why yet, but our future lies within the wood, our adventure together has only just begun…"

Rosie leant forward stroking the silky long white mane. As she looked ahead she could see the shadow of them on the ground. She put her arms around his neck and gave him a hug knowing she must be the luckiest girl in the world to have her very own magic Unicorn friend.

She stroked his smooth creamy fur, leant forward and whispered into his ear, "Image, things don't get much better than this."